a Belladonna Ink novel

Her Hometown Girl

Lorelie Brown

D1096898

RIPTIDE
PUBLISHING

Riptide Publishing
PO Box 1537
Burnsville, NC 28714
www.riptidepublishing.com

This is a work of fiction. Names, characters, places, and incidents are either the product of the author's imagination or are used fictitiously. Any resemblance to actual persons living or dead, business establishments, events, or locales is entirely coincidental. All person(s) depicted on the cover are model(s) used for illustrative purposes only.

Her Hometown Girl
Copyright © 2017 by Lorelie Brown

Cover art: L.C. Chase, lcchase.com/design.htm
Editor: Sarah Lyons
Layout: L.C. Chase, lcchase.com/design.htm

All rights reserved. No part of this book may be reproduced or transmitted in any form or by any means, electronic or mechanical, including photocopying, recording, or by any information storage and retrieval system without the written permission of the publisher, and where permitted by law. Reviewers may quote brief passages in a review. To request permission and all other inquiries, contact Riptide Publishing at the mailing address above, at Riptidepublishing.com, or at marketing@riptidepublishing.com.

ISBN: 978-1-62649-647-7

First edition
September, 2017

Also available in ebook:
ISBN: 978-1-62649-646-0

a Belladonna Ink novel

Her Hometown *Girl*

Lorelie Brown

RIPTIDE
PUBLISHING

To every woman who's been made to feel less than.
You're not.

And to my loves.

table of

Contents

chapter

One

TANSY

*I*t turns out that getting a tattoo hurts. I expected a sting, sure. But getting a flu shot isn't a big deal—it's the soreness the next day that actually hurts.

Yeah, getting inked isn't like that. It's a thousand wasps attacking my skin as a Hitachi Magic Wand vibrates my toes off my foot.

"You okay?" my tattoo artist asks, but she doesn't stop what she's doing. Cai. Her name is Cai. I met her almost two hours ago, when I walked into Belladonna Ink based on Yelp reviews.

"I'm miserable."

"Do you want me to stop?" I hear the amusement in her voice. She scrubs another lick of fire down the center of my calf. "Just warning you, if you take a break and then get going again, pretty much everyone agrees it hurts worse."

"Aren't you a pile of sunshine?"

"Can sunshine pile? Isn't the expression 'a ray of sunshine'?"

I smash my cheek against the chair's support ring thingy. Paper crinkles. "Is this like food service where I shouldn't tell you how much I hate you because you'll spit in my soup? If I tell you how I really feel, will you draw a poop emoji on me?"

"No, because you'll walk around for the rest of your life telling everyone who'll listen that I drew that shit."

"This is true." I blow out a long, shaky breath and am mortified to realize my nose is snotty and I'm holding back tears. Not surprised, but still embarrassed.

It's been a long day.

It's been a long, horrible, no-good, very bad day.

I slept in until eight, and that has probably been the best part of my day. Only twelve hours ago, and an entire lifetime. Two hours after that was mostly okay: brunch with my future mother-in-law and my maid of honor and a couple of others. Jody wasn't with us because she'd wanted to get in a long run before the rich food of the reception. All as expected. Then the makeup artists and hairdressers showed up, and there was still no sign of Jody.

I didn't start getting anxious until I was staring out the window as the hairdresser swept up my long curls and piled them on my head. Jody wasn't answering my texts. I wish I could have said it wasn't like her. I couldn't. A few stories below, I could see hotel staff was setting up for our event. All the chairs were out already, and a florist swagged satin and arranged white roses. The red carpet had been unrolled across the sand, leading toward the waves.

I was already in my wedding dress.

As soon as my hair was done, I slipped out the back door of the suite, down the hallway, and up two floors to Jody's room. The door wasn't closed. Jody's neon-orange leggings were jammed in the way. I picked them up and push the door open slowly.

I saw every inch of penis plunging into her.

After that, it was all over but the shouting. Well, telling Jody's family too. At least I didn't have to tell mine. And naturally Jody bailed, leaving me alone to tell everyone what had happened.

She's lucky I didn't tell them all about why it was canceled. So freaking lucky.

I sent the bar staff home, told the florists to deliver everything to a nearby synagogue, and stiffed the caterer. Maybe I'll feel bad about that tomorrow. Maybe I won't.

The ginger-pubed baby-faced catering assistant had stiffed Jody plenty, after all.

My tears leak into the paper lining of the face rest, making it translucent.

"Why so much lace?" Cai asks.

I wonder if she senses the changes in my body, even through her machine and latex gloves.

The design we agreed on circles the top of my calf with an intricately lined lace pattern gathered around a cluster of pink and purple tulips.

"I was in a wedding dress a few hours ago."

Cai's surprise is in her hesitation. The needle lifts. "Oh yeah?"

It's that asking-but-not-asking thing that people do when they want to hear gossip but aren't sure if you want to share. "Beautiful dress. Heavy satin with swags and just the right amount of Swarovski crystals."

"Do you count those in individual crystals or in square inches covered?"

I crane my neck so I can look over my shoulder at her. I don't see snark in her expression.

Her eyes are dark enough to make them a little unreadable. She has gunmetal gray shadow swiped over crease-free lids, but it doesn't look like she spends a lot of time on makeup. Her mouth is held in a soft smile. If she's mocking me, she's hiding it well.

"I don't know. It had them here." I wave a hand over my torso. "Like a belt. But the thing is, I didn't like it. Not one bit. I wanted boho lace. Gobs of lace and something that only went to my calves. Something that's actually appropriate for a beach wedding."

"Is that where it's going to be? The wedding?" She asks so casually.

This is going to be my future for a while, and I can't help but imagine everyone tiptoeing around me. Not much is going to be point-blank like this, though. I don't have that many close friends.

"That's where it was supposed to be. Two hours ago." I lift my wrist and check my watch, ignoring all the flashing alerts from social media. "No, wait, three hours ago."

"Holy shit." She raises the tattoo machine again and stares at me. Our gazes catch. Her mouth is open a little. The line of her bottom teeth is a perfect curve except for one crooked canine on the left. It tips inward as if it's trying to hide in her mouth. "I thought . . . I thought you had the dress on today for, like, a fitting."

"Nope."

"Dude."

"Yeah." I blink back sudden tears. They go away almost as easily as they appeared.

I wait for her to keep going. Ask what happened. Why I'm not on my way to the Big Sur honeymoon that's bought and paid for. Where my bride is—unless she's reading me wrong and is wondering if I lost a groom. Air gathers in my lungs, and I can't tell if I want to talk or if I want to scream. Maybe I want to wail like a baby.

"Why were you wearing a dress you hated?"

Well, there's an option I wasn't expecting. It's enough to shake me sideways. I use my held breath to hiss through my teeth when she drops her gaze to my leg and goes back to work. "Jody's mom—Jody is, was my fiancée—Marta, paid for my dress and Jody's tux. She wanted us to match styles. Fabrics. Plus she likes bling."

"But you're not a fan."

I shake my head, then realize she might not be looking at any part of me other than my calf. At least, I kind of hope she's not. Concentration is a good thing. Since this is going on me permanently and all. "I'm about as anti-bling as possible. But I did it. Wore it. I figured it was a little thing so everyone would be happy."

"Everyone but you."

"That's the problem." One of the problems. My crushing neuroses, my fear of abandonment, my poor communication skills, and everything else that made me ripe for Jody's particular style of manipulation. That's a pretty big part of the problem too. Plus the aforementioned caterer banging. Problem. Yeah.

"Did you leave her at the altar? Please tell me you did. That would be badass."

I have a sudden, explicit memory of the gray-haired woman who passed us in the hallway at the exact moment Jody screamed she "wouldn't have to act out" if I were "more understanding." I cried and told her I understood perfectly how penises work. Not exactly what I'd call badass. That woman held her fluffy golden puppy closer to her chest and hustled three rooms down.

"Not quite the altar. We weren't going to have one anyway. The beach-wedding thing. An archway covered in flowers."

"Sounds beautiful."

"The flowers had crystals on them."

"You're shitting me."

"We are poop free." I laugh because my only other option is to start sobbing. "Jody and her mom wrapped the stems in crystals and glued drops to petals. I mean, they didn't do it themselves. They got the florist to do it and paid plenty."

"Aren't flowers pretty enough?"

"It was all I could do to convince them not to spray-paint them gold."

"Spray-painting flowers?"

"It's a thing. A Pinterest thing." I run my hands up under my hair. It's still stiff with product. My scalp burns when I catch and tug strands. "Don't get me wrong, I had two different Pinterest boards for the wedding, but Jody had ten. Weirdest butch I ever met. Whatever. She had to control everything. It's probably my fault for letting her."

"It doesn't work that way." Cai looks up and flashes a tight smile at me. "Abusers take what they need, whether you give it or not."

My skin flashes first ice-cold and then prickles hot. "She's not an abuser." Because that would mean I was abused. "She never once hit me or pushed me or really anything like that."

Cai's touch is soothing as she uses a paper towel to wipe away blood and ink. "Okay," she says so gently that I feel like she's patronizing me. "Sorry. I didn't mean to make assumptions."

I think of a hundred small memories and moments at once, and then they're gone and I breathe again. "Yeah."

"Here we go," she says, pouring foaming liquid all over my leg and then wiping it again. "You're all done."

"I am?" I'm both stunned and relieved in a blink of time. "Can I see?"

"Sure. Come here."

She leads me to a full-length mirror at the end of the short hallway of stalls. Some of them have curtains pulled, but in the next-to-last one is a girl with short-short hair getting an old-fashioned anchor on her shoulder. She winks at me.

I scurry away. I'm standing in front of the mirror, staring blankly at my reflection before I realize my shoulders are tight and my chest is locked against air because I'm expecting Cai to snark at me, every word covered in passive-aggressive poison. *Like them butch?* she'll ask me.

Except it's not really Cai I expect to start in on me. It's Jody who'd say things like that. Who *has* said things like that when a waitress was a little too friendly. Then she'd told me the waitress was only looking for a good tip and I shouldn't be so naïve.

I rub my temple. It doesn't do anything to get at the swirling thoughts in my head.

"Do you like it?" Cai has her arms folded over her chest, leaning back against a half wall papered in textured red. Her button-down is crisp. The suspenders outline the subtle curves of her body. Her long black ponytail lies over the front of her shoulder and brushes her wrist.

She is everything too cool for school. Everyone I wanted to be but never managed. I'm too much of a mess, too hungry for approval and love. The thing is, I can't remember if I've always been like this. Why did I put up with Jody for so long? Something has to be wrong with me.

But the cocked angle of Cai's head trips my feelings-on-alert trigger. The degree she's holding her shoulders. She's anxious. She wants me to like the tattoo she's inked into my skin.

"It's gorgeous," I assure her.

And it is. My badge, my symbol of never giving up on myself again. No matter what it takes. The black lace curls around my skin as if it's real. The tulips are vibrant and bursting with color. I point my toes and flex my calf, watching it move. From every angle, it's amazing.

Cai gives me a rundown on caring for it, everything I need to do and not do. I listen carefully, but at the same time there's a creeping dread slipping in around the edges of my brain.

"Are you okay?" she asks. She touches my forearm.

It's the first skin-to-skin contact we've had. Everything else has had safety barriers between us.

More than that, I think maybe it's the first time I've had skin-to-skin contact that wasn't Jody in a long time. A very long time. If I didn't keep myself carefully to myself, life always got so hard. Jody made sure of it. And then all my friends are actually Jody's friends, and they would never hug me or lean on me. I didn't think I wanted them to, but the way my body cries out for more must mean I need it. I need someone.

I'm so alone.

"I don't know if I want to go home," I blurt out. A different kind of truth but still pretty terrifying to hear coming out of my mouth.

Two

CAI

I can't take a wounded bird home. I can't fucking do it. "Do you feel like you won't be safe?"

I don't know how I want her to answer. With the truth, of course. With some element of assurance that will let me off the hook too, if I'm honest with myself.

She gives it to me. One of her hands flutters in a no-big-deal flick. "No, it's fine. It's just that I'm conflict-avoidant, so that's what I'm doing. Avoiding conflict."

It sounds like she's repeating something she's said—or heard—a hundred times.

I don't get to give more than the slightest attention to how cute this girl is. She's a client, and she's got enough emotional baggage packed up to need two valets. She doesn't need me creeping on her.

Tansy cried through the second half of the session, so her hazel eyes are red-rimmed and her button nose is pink at the tip. I'm a sick fuck to find her adorable like this, but there it is. I want to hide her away from the world and make sure she never meets an unkind soul again.

Which is exactly the reason I should stay away.

She's a slip of nothing. Only about five foot at most, which makes her a full six inches shorter than me. If I wore my big boots, the difference would be even more noticeable. I want to cup the back of her head, touch the ginger strands that look like a fuzzy cloud to see if those strands are soft or like twine. If I shelter her from the storm, I might remember what it feels like to be strong.

Instead I do nothing, say nothing, and lead her back to my cubicle. I dress the tattoo in a protective bandage. It's always strange to know my art is going to get up and walk away into the world, and this time is no different.

"Touch-ups are on the house, always are," I say, and she nods like a star pupil. "*Anything* you don't like, come back and see me."

"You sound serious."

"I am." I reach toward her leg, but I don't touch her. I circle the air instead, but it doesn't matter. I still know what her skin feels like. "My goal is for you to be happy with what I made of you for the rest of your life. When you're eighty-seven and rocking out on the retirement home's beach trip and someone asks you about it, I want you to give my name with pride."

"I'm way more of a hot tub girl," she says with a smile that sneaks its way past her day's heartbreak. "Or ponds. Or creeks. The ocean is too freaky for me."

"Me too. There's no jellyfish in a creek."

"Exactly."

But as I'm grinning at her, reminding myself that this girl has more than enough on her plate and that I have no interest in this kind of chick, I hear commotion at the front end of the shop. To be exact, it's a loud voice with a tyrannical tone that sets my back teeth to grinding. "What is that?"

All the color is gone from Tansy's face. Her formerly pink cheeks are the pale cold white of porcelain. The curve of her bottom lip is shallow and drawn taut. "That's Jody."

As if saying those words has cracked her, she scrambles off my chair and dives for the messenger bag she left hanging on a hook. She fishes out a phone in a pink camo case. "Stupid Find My Phone! I didn't know she had the password. How long has she had that?"

"You seem kind of freaked out."

She flashes me a wide-eyed look of panic that's at odds with what comes out of her mouth. "It's fine. Jody's going to be upset, but I practically left her at the altar. She has every right to be emotional.

It looks like she was trying to reach me, so she's probably been worried about me too."

I . . . have no idea what to do with that. She's the biggest ball of anxiety I've seen since the client who had a phobia of needles and ended up having a panic attack.

Tansy gathers her messenger bag and slings it over her shoulders. The strap rests between her breasts, molding her silk, sleeveless blouse to her figure. She has surprisingly large breasts for such a small frame.

She also has an artery pounding under the delicately thin skin at her temple. When she licks her bottom lip, it barely leaves a sheen, as if her mouth is dry as stone. "Do I pay you directly? Or up front?"

"Front of the house." I wave toward the general area where I can hear Jody bitching.

"I have every fucking right to be here." Her voice spikes above the velvet curtains dividing the tattoo benches. "My wife is here."

"I'm not her wife," Tansy mutters, but then it's like she remembers I'm here. She blinks and gives me a great smile that I've done nothing to earn. If I didn't look too closely, I might think nothing was wrong.

I follow her down the narrow, short hall. Jody spots her before she manages to step into the foyer. "Tansy! Where have you been?"

Tansy walks to the counter without looking at her fiancée and hands a credit card to Nayla, who's working the front desk and register. "I've been here. Add thirty percent tip," she says to Nayla.

"I've been worried about you."

It's a spooky echo of the words Tansy had said to me moments ago. Goose bumps walk across my shoulders.

Jody is tall and coolly femme. She's slender enough that there's a circle of taut skin at the base of her neck between her collarbones that reminds me of Robin Wright.

My crush on Claire Underwood dies a fiery death right then and there.

"Maybe you should have thought about that before humping that guy four hours before our wedding."

My gaze jumps to Nayla's. We both have wide did-you-hear-that eyes. Tansy is still keeping her face tipped away from Jody. The line of her shoulders is so tight that they're creeping toward her ears as if she's trying to ward off a blow.

"You know how I feel about publicly airing unpleasantness." Jody's voice is calm. Weirdly so. If I'd been caught doing the deed on my wedding day, I think I'd be a hell of a lot more upset. But then, I don't know their dynamic. Maybe this is the fifth time they've been through this dance. All things considered, I'm pretty helpless. This isn't my fight to pick.

I lean against the glass-and-chrome counter and shove my hands in my pockets. "Thanks for the tip." Considering the cost of the tat, it's pretty good money.

"It's worth every penny," Tansy says with complete sincerity. She manages to meet my gaze for a second before bouncing away, looking back down at her purse and making an event of putting her card away.

"Oh," Jody says on a mouthful of sigh. I think she's just noticed the bandage. "What did you do to yourself, Tansy?"

"It's my body and I've always wanted a tattoo."

"You've never mentioned it to me."

"You've made your disdain for tattoos more than clear."

Jody rocks back on her heels as if she's astonished. Her blue chambray button-down is impeccably pressed. Whatever hunting and worrying she's been doing over Tansy has been quite tidily done. "Just because I think they're trashy shouldn't matter. I would never, ever tell you what to do."

If Tansy believes that, she's in deeper than I thought. Control drips off this woman in the way she's trying to be charming and utterly failing at it.

"I'm tired, Jody. I need to rest."

"Naturally. We'll go home and talk for a while and then you can sleep."

"There's nothing to discuss. I'm done with you."

"I know. And I know it's my fault." When Tansy looks at her, she arranges her mouth into a disappointed frown that wasn't there a moment ago. "But at the very least we have to figure out how to separate our lives. All the logistics. And I want to tell you how very, very deep I've been delving about how terrible I've been. How reckless I've been in my choices. I'm an awful person, Tansy."

"You're not," she says, and I want to physically throw myself between them. Take Tansy's shoulders and shake her.

As it is, I can't keep my mouth shut. "Think maybe you should try throwing an 'I'm sorry' in there?"

Tansy's head whips from Jody to me so fast that a piece of hair catches at her mouth. She shoves it away.

"This isn't any of your business," Jody says in a cutting sneer that drags Tansy's gaze back to her.

"But you didn't. You didn't say sorry." Tansy's eyes are wide.

"You know how sorry I am." Jody holds out her hands, palms up. They're rock steady. "I am filled with regret."

I lift an eyebrow. "Regret from fucking that dude or from getting caught?" This is kind of fun.

This time Jody appeals straight to Tansy. "This is why we need privacy. Let's go home. I promise I'll sleep on the couch."

My impulse gets the best of me. I push off the counter and lean into the blonde with the haughty attitude. Holier-than-thou shit always gets my back up. "She's not going anywhere with you."

"Cai, it's okay." Tansy puts her hand in the middle of my back. The touch is feather soft but enough to make me realize how stiff I've become. "I have to pack a bag and get my cat. It'll be fine."

We're strangers. I don't know her. She doesn't know me. There's a great, vast nothingness between us, and I could throw all the guesses and suppositions in the world in there and not fill it up. I've been here before, in a place where not knowing is worse than the truth. "Are you sure?"

But, at the same time, I don't know what I'm doing. There's no way I can take this stranger home with me. It's not even about some amorphous worry that she'll rob my apartment. It's about what I'm not capable of—the kind of long-term healing that Tansy desperately needs. I'm running from my own demons, after all.

"I'm positive," she says, and I decide to let her have her lie.

"Thanks for the tip," I say again. I shove my hands in the back pockets of my jeans to keep from doing anything stupid. "Don't forget to come back for the touch-up." I hear myself making it nonoptional. I hope she realizes what I mean.

"Thanks. For everything." For a moment I think she'd going to hug me, but then she gives a tight smile to Jody instead. "Let's go."

Their walk out the door is a dance. Jody's fingers at the small of her back. Tansy stepping away. Jody tries for her shoulder instead, and then they're out of sight.

I stare at the closed door longer than I want to admit.

chapter

Three

Tansy

Breaking apart a couple takes even more work than I expected. Finding Jody in bed with that guy had almost felt like a relief. At last. Here it was. The thing I could point to and explain why a relationship that should have been so right was pure misery.

She was cheating all along. Of course I must have realized on some level.

Jody spends hours explaining how lost and pressured she'd felt. She'd crumpled under my expectations.

I didn't know it was so much to ask her to support me and love me.

She keeps me up until 3 a.m. before she finally admits that we have to sleep sometime.

When I try to remind her about her promise to sleep on the couch, she acts like she never said anything like that. My memory is failing me under all this stress. Maybe I'm wrong.

"I'll sleep on the couch, then."

"You won't get any real rest." She's standing in the bathroom we've shared for eighteen months. One of her fists rests on the edge of the raised sink bowl. "You'll toss and turn."

"I'll be fine." My eyes are so bleary, it hurts to blink.

"Here, take a Xanax at least." She grabs the bottle from the medicine cabinet and shakes one into her palm.

"Those are yours."

"And I'm sleeping in the bed, where I'll sleep like a log."

Sleep like a log when we're less than twelve hours away from what should have been our wedding. I can't understand her.

"Fine," I tell her. I take the pill and toss it back. I'm going to sleep either way so it doesn't really matter.

I hold the small, stuffed bear that's been with me since my childhood in Idaho and shuffle to the pale-gray sectional. The blanket from the back of the couch is thin but warm when I nestle into it. Tears burn my cheeks. I hold down the sobs that I could make, because I don't want Jody to come back. I want space. I want to breathe. I'm not sure I'll ever breathe right again. When I think the combination of my silence and snotty nose will choke me, I roll over so that my face is buried in the throw pillows.

And, the thing is, I don't think I'm crying over my relationship. I want to be free. I want myself back. I cry because I can—because it's not my job anymore to be the calm, rational person that Jody always demanded.

It hurts to realize again that I'm human. With human feelings that have been hidden for so long I'm not sure if it's best to wipe my eyes as I cry or if that will make things worse. I've forgotten how to cry.

I drop into sleep like a pebble into a well.

I jerk out of sleep gasping.

"No, no, it's okay," a familiar voice says. Jody.

I wipe a hand across my eyes. My sight won't clear. I think it's the crying that's left my eyes swollen. Or maybe the pill. "Jody, we have to sleep."

"I couldn't."

"What time is it?"

"Five."

Two hours after she finally let me go to sleep. I can't think. I am fog. "I have to sleep."

"You can't leave me."

"I don't want to be with you anymore." It's my clarion call. The one thing I kept saying over and over last night, between the explanations, between her justification.

"I don't know what I'll do." She's sitting on the edge of the couch, her hip pinning my ribs in. She takes my hand, wrapping her fingers around mine. "If you go . . . I might as well be dead. Maybe I will be."

I don't say anything, which could seem awful to some people, but I know from the other times that there's no right answer. If I act like I don't care despite the adrenaline surging down my useless stick limbs, she'll flip to rage. If I take her veiled threats seriously, we'd end up with her mocking me for needing safe spaces and too much sensitivity training.

My mouth feels like it's been wiped down with cotton wadding, so dry I can barely swallow.

"You won't leave me." Jody pets my hair back. "We're good together. Everyone says so."

I rub my tongue over my lips. It's hard to line up words. "I want to go." I can't think past the basics.

"You don't."

"I do."

"After everything I've done for you. Everything I've given you?" There's a light on in the bedroom, just enough to let me see the shape of Jody's face but not her eyes. I don't trust her if I can't see her eyes. She's cold like a Russian saint and just as hard. Her grip on my hand tightens. My bones grind together.

"You're hurting me."

"You're hurting *me*," she echoes, pinching my fingers tighter.

Tears well in my scratchy, swollen eyes. "Please."

"Always with the tears. I'm not hurting you. I love you."

Aren't these my bones? She pushes my hair away from my face and kisses me. I don't kiss her back, but I don't pull away either. She'll only get more upset with me. Her hold on my hand loosens at last. It's only when she pushes my shoulders down that I realize I've been trying to curl up and get away. I *am* away. I'm floating even though I'm lying flat.

Gyoza meows from somewhere else in the apartment. I think she must be on her perch in the dining room. He likes the window overlooking the pool.

I guess Jody is still kissing me. She's flat on me. Her thighs straddle my thigh and she rubs. She buries her face against my cleavage, and the irony almost kills me. My breast are sensitive. During tough times, I had to beg her to touch me there. Told her how much more eager for sex I'd be.

She does it now. Not then.

I stare at the ceiling. My hands are flush against the couch cushions. For a second I think the fabric's damp, and then I realize that my palms are sweaty.

She cups my breast, her hand beneath my V-neck shirt. The individual brands of her fingertips are made of sandpaper.

Any minute now, she'll notice that I'm not here. I'm not with her. I'm so far away that each long, slow blink moves me back and forth across galaxies.

She grips my shoulder tightly. I make a noise like a whimper. I guess it hurts. She intertwines my fingers with hers and pushes them down her cotton shorts. She's wet. I try to pull my hand away, but she doesn't let go.

In a little bit, she's done.

With a gasp that's nearly a cry, she collapses on me. Her knees push between mine. Her head rests on my chest.

Outside a car door slams shut. The downstairs neighbors are home. I hold my breath and wonder when Jody will get off me. How much space is in the universe. There are molecules between her and me. I wish there were more.

I wish I hadn't taken that pill.

"You see?" Jody touches a single, wet finger to my sternum and pets a sticky path to the neckline of my T-shirt. "We'll work this out."

"I'm going away," I promise, and then sleep swallows me.

chapter

Four

CAI

I pretty much thought that I wasn't going to see her again, so it's probably a good thing that she's looking at a framed picture when I step into the waiting area. It gives me a chance to get a good look at her. Take everything in.

It's the riotous pile of her curls that draws my attention first. The sun is sliding sideways through the front window and the orange glow of sunset has made her a halo. She lifts both hands and shoves her fingers into the mass to give it a shake. She pulls back out the way she went in rather than stroke through to the ends.

Six weeks is a long time and also kind of a blink. She's exactly the same, this person I've seen once, and yet I think there's something wrong with her. Her oversized shirt is blue plaid that almost manages to hide the gray pallor of her skin. There are purple shadows at the inner corners of her eyes.

"I wasn't sure you'd come back," I tell her.

She jumps even though she's come to the shop looking for me. "You thought your work was that good? I wouldn't need a touch-up?"

"No." I push my hands into the pockets of my shorts. "I knew if you stayed with that woman, you would eventually pretend you'd never even seen a tattoo machine. Much less sat for one."

"Whoa. Why are you being so mean?" It's a little fucked up, but the shadows under her eyes make their hazel-brown color even richer. Her lashes are pale and short.

And all this is me trying to distract myself from my truth. I like her vulnerability way more than I should. "I don't know."

"If I hadn't already, I wouldn't be getting ink from you. This is not good customer service." Her jaw is sharply square and even more so when she clenches.

"Yeah, I know." I rub the back of my neck. I have my hair in a high ponytail today, which works with my tank top. Skylar would give me crap about looking sloppy if it weren't for the shorts being leather. "It's been a tough couple days. I shouldn't have said that. Come on back and we'll take a look at you."

As she follows me to my station, I can practically feel annoyance radiating from her like heat.

"Not that it's your business, but I did leave her. I packed my stuff the next day."

"Good. I'm glad to hear that." Not platitudes. Not a polite lie. For some reason I really do feel weight lift off my shoulders. "Got your own place now?"

"Kind of. I'm pretty lucky; one of my students' parents is letting me use an apartment they own. I'm still looking for something permanent though. It's all so freaking expensive."

"The market is rough lately. I'm sure you'll find somewhere soon."

"Tell me about it. I could go back to school for as much as some places are charging." She tosses a small tote onto my extra chair. "And it's not like I enjoyed college that much the first time around."

"I enjoyed it too much. So much that I dropped out." I pat the big, padded tattoo throne. "Up you go."

"I have to admit, I thought about it like a dozen or a hundred times or so." She gives me a slightly embarrassed look from under her brows. "It was Jody who got me through. Not the academic stuff, I was fine with that. I was so lonely. I'm from Idaho, and the adjustment to Cal State Fullerton was overwhelming."

"And Jody rescued you?"

"We lived in the same hall. She . . ." Tansy trails off, looking past me into her memories. Then her mouth twists into a wry smile. "She set herself up as my rescuer, told me no one would ever understand me the way she did, and they wouldn't want me anyway. I shouldn't keep romanticizing her. So say the self-help books."

"Self-help books talk a good line." I like the way she smells today, like fresh flowers and rain. "It's a hell of a lot harder to live. If they weren't, I wouldn't be nearly as screwed up as I am. Maybe I'd even settle down with a nice woman and a Subaru and a couple mastiffs."

"A Subaru and dogs?" She laughs. "You've read the Lesbian Bible one too many times. You don't have to live the stereotype, you know."

"I'm actually bi," I say in mock-seriousness. "Throws the gaydar off every time."

"No, I mean, yeah, I thought you were gay of some sort, but that was mostly wish fulfillment because I thought maybe you were flirting with me last time I was here. Before Jody showed up at—" She breaks off abruptly, clamping her mouth shut. She goes so red that the apples of her cheeks circle round to white while the rest of her is scalding. "Sorry. Rambling. I know it's annoying."

"No, it isn't." I grasp her upper arm. She's shaking, and hard. "It's cute."

"You don't have to lie."

"I'm not."

She's looking down at her lap, where her hands are locked together. Her shaking subsides before she manages to look up at me. "Honest?"

"Cross my heart."

She takes a long, slow breath that lifts and lowers her shoulders. "Thank you."

Her bravery is so in my face that it's startling. I rub the arm I'm holding, keeping the move as brisk and reassuring as I can manage. I don't do relationships well. Connection is difficult—but it's exactly what this girl needs, which means I'm exactly who should stay away from her. "Lay down and let me see your leg."

She's facedown practically before I can blink. I fight the urge to call her a good girl, and settle for patting her shoulder. She's like petting a baby duck or a puppy. Makes me want to nuzzle her.

"Mostly it's perfect," she says, and for a minute I think she's poking around inside my head and telling me this temptation is okay. Except of course she's talking about her tattoo. "I didn't heal well on the left and now there's some light bits?"

"I see what you mean." I lay a finger on about an inch of lighter gray among the black. "Right here."

"Yeah. Can you fix it?"

"Totally. You head to the front again, and I'll get everything sanitized. Let you know when I'm ready for you."

"Awesome," she squeaks and then she does this amazingly, mind-numbingly sexy/cute butt wiggle.

I deserve a Nobel fucking Anti-Sex Prize for not gripping that soft bubble with both hands and squeezing tight. "Right," I manage to choke out. I clear my throat and repeat myself. "Right. Off with you."

"I'm really happy. I was freaked out that I'd done something wrong and it wouldn't be fixable and it's so beautiful. I would be so mad at myself if it was ruined." She seems to recognize that she's doing that rambling thing, because her fingers lift to her mouth and she blushes again. It's not as fierce as last time.

I still want to kiss her, and that could not be a more terrible idea. I'm too hard for her, too cold. Far too cold.

I send her off to wait and rabbit through all the sterilization that will keep both her and me safe. The whole time, I turn the possibilities over and over in my mind. Six weeks since an aborted wedding probably isn't long enough for her to be over her terrible-sounding ex, but maybe that's okay. I'm not exactly looking for forever anyway. A drink and some flirting and seeing what possibly happens from there . . . It's not out of the realm of things that could come true.

I'm not built for complicated. I know that. But she probably can't handle complicated. I may even be doing her something of a favor by helping her get into the world again without expecting too much.

Once my gear is ready, I go back out to the waiting area to collect her. Only this time she's not studying the art. She's sitting and waiting and watching for me.

And, Christ, the way her face lights up when she smiles is a thing of magic. My fingers curl with the need to touch that smile. How can she be so sweet? So happy? If I had been the one to walk in on my fiancée boning some dude, I'd still be a rage ball. Instead, she worries that she's the one who's fucked up the tattoo—not the way most customers would pin the blame on me.

"All set," I tell her.

"Great," she pipes and hops up. "I hope it doesn't hurt as bad as last time."

I usher her back to my station. "If it does, at least it'll be over soon. Much less to do this time."

"Awesome."

She lies facedown and indeed it's all over in no time. I darken up the smudges and have to round out one too-sharp curve. Over all, I'm pretty stoked with how her ink turned out. It's less than fifteen minutes of touch-up, but once I finish and she sits up, there are tears in her eyes.

I hide my grin as I snap off my latex gloves. "You really do have a low pain tolerance, don't you?"

She blinks away the tears with a sniffle or two. "I guess so. I've never really tested it out before."

"No more tats for you? You're not going to get ink fever and be back in a couple weeks?"

"No way." A tear breaks loose and skates over her rounded cheek even though she's smiling. "Don't get me wrong, I love this one. But no more. Ever."

I don't even try to resist my urge and wipe her tear away with my thumb. My fingertips rest on her soft neck, and I think I can feel her heart racing. Or maybe that's my own pounding pulse. "Then how will I see you again?"

"Do you want to?" She's motionless all over, staring at me, and it's only then that I realize how much she's usually moving. Her hands flutter and her shoulders shift.

"Yeah. I do."

She bursts into movement again, ducking her head and using both hands to shove her curls behind her ears. "I could stop by?"

"Or we could go on a date." She's freaking adorable.

"A date would be good. When?"

"How about now?" I'm not sure where the impulse comes from, but I decide to follow it. "I'm on the schedule until ten, but I don't have any appointments."

She slides off the chair and hooks her bag over her shoulder. "I'm ready for whatever."

It shouldn't be enticing, but I have lots of ideas for what *whatever* could entail. I put up a finger. "Wait here real quick."

I duck in the back room to tell Skylar that I'm heading out. She doesn't mind. I keep enough customers rolling in that I can get some leeway when I want it. And when it comes to Tansy, I definitely want it.

Tansy waits outside the front door of the shop, turned away. She's wearing a Henley and shorts and that blue plaid. Now that I know she's from Idaho, it's got a different feel than most girls I see running around in plaid shirts. This is probably something she's worn all her life. When she was a little girl with pale-red hair in pigtails and rosy cheeks, she'd have worn the same thing. I bet she's the type who went tromping through mud and just kept going.

When she spots me, she turns and smiles. I love that smile. She looks joyous to see me, which makes me feel pretty damn good in turn.

"Hi," she says, and then she blushes. "Sorry."

"For what?"

"Being goofy." She shakes her head in a way that I'm coming to recognize is more a way of scolding herself into stopping whatever she's talking about. "Where are we going?"

"My favorite dive bar."

"You Californians are so cute." She falls into step beside me. "You don't know what a dive bar is until you've seen a bar in Salmon. It's not a dive bar just because they don't have a dance floor."

"I don't know. This place is pretty old-school."

"Does it have a moose head on the wall?"

"No, but it does have a giant mounted blue fin tuna hanging from the ceiling."

She narrows her eyes as if she's seriously considering the qualifications, but I see her hiding a smile in the tucks of her cheeks. "I reserve the right to declare Whiskey Willy's superior."

"Seriously? That's the name of the joint?"

"Yup. It's right on Main Street."

I laugh. "Is it actually Main Street? Belladonna Ink is on Main too. I bet they look way different."

"The name's on the signs. Cross my heart and hope to die." She flashes me the cutest fucking grin. It lives in the way her eyes sparkle under the setting sun. I want the right to curl a hand over the back of her neck and drag her mouth to mine.

I settle for saying, "You're adorable."

She jumps so hard, it's almost as if I told her that I think she kicks puppies. "What?"

"You're cute." I think I've said something wrong, or something that hits a weird point in her brain or memories. I guess? I stop walking, since we're at Mikey's. "Your features are arranged in a pleasing manner. Is that not okay? Did I go too far?"

"No, it's fine," comes out of her mouth, but her eyes are so wide and she's standing on the tiptoes of one foot. It's almost a sprinter's starting stance, like she's going to dash away.

I don't want to push her too much, so I hold the wooden door open but step back so she's got plenty of room. "Here. Grab a seat anywhere you want."

chapter

Five

TANSY

The doorway to the place is draped in shadows, and I can't see much of the room beyond. Cai is looking at me, but trying not to look too hard. I know that expression. It's one where I've done something totally batshit crazy and she doesn't know what to do. I get that at work sometimes, when I say something weird and Courtney and Imogene don't know how to respond. The past two weeks since school started up again have been hard. I've been saying a lot of stupid stuff. But it's been better than sitting alone in my new apartment.

So naturally my heartbeat shoots into an astronomically fast pattern. Because I'm kinda crazy, even when I don't mean to be. I'm still smiling. I tuck a bit of hair behind my ear and go through the door.

She called me cute. Adorable. That's not a bad thing. It's not something that ought to make me feel like puking. It's not the cute type of puking either, where it's all about butterfly wings in my stomach or something like that. The back of my neck is prickling, and I feel sweat at the base of my spine.

I am a fucked-up pile of neuroses still.

This is Jody's fault. It's Jody still taking from me when I thought I was moving on. I'm going to screw up this thing with Cai before it even gets started. I don't want to die alone.

I pick a table near the big plate-glass windows that are folded open to an insanely beautiful sunset. "I like the pier against the colors."

"Yeah." Cai sits down across from me. "The contrast gives me perspective. Like, those aren't just some random colors."

"It's a focus point, something to look at inside the whole picture." The orange and pink and red streak across the horizon, blending the ocean and sky together. Cirrus clouds are reflected in the waves beneath. "I went to the Grand Canyon once, and it was the weirdest thing. I pinged back and forth between feeling like this crack in the ground is no big deal and being almost lightheaded with how big and intimidating and scary it was. I could only take in little bits of it at a time."

"How old were you?"

"Seventeen. The summer before I left for college. We went on a family road trip."

"Oh my god, family road trips were my idea of hell." Cai shudders dramatically. "Did you guys rent a van? We always took the whole family, so it was me and my cousins like five rows away from my parents. I was so at their mercy."

I laugh. "No, we just had Mom and Dad and my brother. Much smaller affair, but Justin did his best to be as annoying as four kids."

"Is he older or younger than you?"

"Younger. Four years younger. He literally did the 'I'm not touching you' gig. I mean, how petty can you be?"

"My cousin Grace once stole all my panties, soaked them in water, and shoved them in the hotel room's freezer." Cai folds her arms on the table, leans in, and tells me like this is a delicious secret. And I'm leaning toward her too. "They froze, but she hadn't noticed that the ice packs for our grandmother's medicine were in there. They got completely wrapped up around each other. Thawing my panties became a family event. I was fucking mortified."

"Oh my god." I'm laughing, even though I feel terrible for it. I cover my mouth with my hand as if that'll keep her feelings from being hurt. I don't think she's sensitive over the story though. The way her eyes are sparking, there's something more to it. "Did you get revenge?"

"No." She shakes her head, her expression solemn. "I would never. And I have no idea how her love letter to Ty Parsons got photocopied and taped up all around school that September."

"You didn't!" I squeal.

"Oh, no. I totally did." She's laughing as much as I'm laughing. "Grace didn't speak to me for six months after that. I can't really blame her."

"You're lucky she *ever* decided to talk to you again."

"Our moms forced us to hash it out." She shrugs. "Family first and all that."

"Are you guys still good?"

"She invited me to dinner two weeks ago, so I think we're fine." She casts me a side-ways glance out the corner of her eyes as she lifts a hand to catch the waitress's attention. Her smile is sly. "I think she keeps her diary locked in a safe though."

And naturally I die laughing again.

The waitress who pops up beside us has a friendly smile. "Is the joke worth sharing?"

"Don't share your secrets with this one," I say as I point at Cai.

"Oh yeah, we all know she's trouble." She pushes a brown braid behind her shoulder. "In more than one way."

"Nope. Not me. You're talking about someone else." Cai folds her hands behind her head, elbows pointing toward the ceiling as she leans as far back in her chair as she can manage. She's deliciously butch, filling up the space as if she deserves the whole world. But then she makes a show of talking out the side of her mouth and faux-whispering. "Shut it, Bonnie. You're going to wreck my chances with the pretty girl."

I giggle. It's not on purpose, and I look down at the lacquered tabletop. Layered beneath plexiglass are handfuls of pretty beach postcards of San Sebastian. Glare shines off a posed blonde's head, and I realize the overhead lights have clicked on.

I'm the pretty girl. I guess.

I mean, I know I am, but... it feels like asking for trouble to admit it. As if the universe would then yank it back and give me a mouthful of sand in exchange for my hubris.

I can't hold back my blush, though. The heat eats up my cheeks and the tips of my ears. "I'll take the house special."

The waitress uses her pen to scratch the back of her neck. "Um, we don't really have any specials. We just kind of do the regular stuff. Like, a daiquiri, mai tai? Or a margarita?"

Shit. I look at Cai, hoping she can't spot my awkwardness, but of course she can. Because—duh—I looked at her with panic scribbled all over me. I rub my hand over the edge between plexiglass and lacquered, shiny wood. "Okay. Yeah. I'll take a daiquiri mai tai."

"Which . . . one?" She glances at Cai as if for help.

I am the stupidest person on the face of the Earth. I cover my eyes with one hand so the words will come spilling out more easily. "I don't drink often. My ex didn't approve. So I've only ever had beer or wine, and she ordered it for us anyway, so I don't really know *what* to order in a place like this."

My cheeks are burning still, and the back of my neck and probably my entire chest all the way down to my sternum too. Because I am one flaming, spiraling ball of social maladjustment.

Cai folds a hand over the one I still have on the table. Her hand's warm and surprisingly rough. Her skin brushing over me reminds me of a cat's tentative kisses. "Do you want wine? They do have some. I could tell you the types, give you a run down."

I lower my hand. Her eyes are dark compassion. There's pain that swims back there, but she's holding it away for me. I want to believe it's not pity, but I'm probably wrong. Maybe pity isn't so bad. Maybe it could grow into something respectable in time. "It's okay. I'd rather . . . I'd rather have a Long Island Iced Tea."

Bonnie's gone, I realize. Not far. She's pulled away to the waitress station a couple of tables away, and she's making busy straightening up a bin of lemon slices and wiping the soda dispenser. I make a mental note to tip her double whatever I spend.

Cai's head tilts and dark hair spills over her cheek. "That's what you want?"

"It's . . . tough?" I want to turn my hand palm side up beneath hers. Is that done? Is it okay? "Back home, everyone pretty much just drank beer or flavored vodka."

When I went too far with Jody, she'd recoil. She's never been fond of public displays of affection. Never. Except those times when she started it, usually because there was someone nearby who she wanted to send a message to. Which . . . sounds absolutely batshit now that I turn it over in my head.

My stomach still churns as I hold my palm up. Cai doesn't pull away. She doesn't lace her fingers through mine the way I'd hoped, but she does trace a circle around the base of my thumb. The churning turns into butterflies.

"A Long Island will have you flat on the floor in about twenty minutes. Is that what you mean by tough?"

"No. Something . . ." I want to cover my face again, but I don't, because I'm working on that whole brave thing everywhere in my life. After all, I'm holding hands with one of the most beautiful women I've ever met. If she were a model, she'd be the type to set trends. "Something old-school cool. What Rhett Butler would order."

"Rhett, huh?" Her lush mouth quirks into a smile, and she flags Bonnie down again. "I know what we need here."

"Ready?" Bonnie hops to it with her pencil hovering over her mini spiral-bound notebook.

"Two Jamesons, two Pappys, and two pours of Macallan."

She cocks an eyebrow and snickers. "You want those shaken or stirred?"

"Each neat, smart-ass."

"You got it, boss." She tucks the pencil behind her ear as she saunters away.

"You come here a lot?"

"Yup." She doesn't seem the least bit guilty or apprehensive about going to a bar often. She also hasn't let go of my hand. "I've got a circle of friends that hangs out here. It helps that it's right down from the shop and still open after we close. They serve a killer ceviche too."

"Yeah?" I perk up and glance around. "I'm always looking for a new source. It's one of my favorite things."

"Japanese food has had the corner on raw fish long enough," she says with an over-played nod. "We should rise up and revolt on behalf of Peruvian food."

"Not that ceviche is technically raw." Crap, that came out in what Jody always called my schoolmarm tone. I pull my hand back to my lap before Cai has a chance to pull away first. Outside the windows, the sun has gone down. It's not quite dark yet, but the gray shadows of dusk are gathering into something that's almost night.

"No?" Cai's voice doesn't have a sharp edge. "It's never cooked though."

"It's cured." I twist my fingers together and worry the bottom hem of my flannel. "It's the citrus juice. It still has to be fresh, but the result is a chemical process."

I'm embarrassing myself, but I just can't seem to shut my mouth, and half of it is my surprise—shock?—that she's not telling me to shut up, not even with her body language. So I go on a little while about the technical properties behind how it works, mostly just to see if she has a line. Not about ceviche, it seems like. It's so weird. No one wants to hear about my random bits of school teacher knowledge. Jody helped me tone that part of myself down and be more interesting.

Unless she didn't. Unless she was actually just ruining me.

The words in my mouth dry up, but it's right as Bonnie arrives with a tray of drinks, so I don't think Cai notices. Or if she does, she's kind and lets it go.

Bonnie lines up three glasses in front of each of us. The first is a pair of squared off, squat tumblers. The next pair are classic shot glasses, and the last set are bell-shaped on a short stem. "Jameson in the tulips, Pappy in the shots, and Macallan neat."

I blink, but that seems to have made sense to Cai. She thanks Bonnie, who disappears as quickly as she came. "What do I do?"

"Whatever you want to."

"You're not going to tell me the rules?"

She tilts her head enough that silky black hair slides over her cheek. The line of her shoulders to her arms to her graceful, long fingers is so relaxed. I don't know if I've ever been that relaxed before in my life. I'm sure I must have been at some point, but it's been a long time. My entire being is a drawn knot. I am made of wire and disappointment.

"There's no rules to booze."

"Why did you pick these three?" I touch the rim of the shot glass. It's full enough that a drop of alcohol clings to the pad of my finger. I lick it away. It's a kiss of fire.

"I like them." She picks up the one in the tumbler. "This one's my favorite scotch."

I grab my tiny glass instead to be contrary. "And Pappy?"

"Pappy Van Winkle is a bourbon. It's a big deal because it's limited release. Hard to get a whole bottle of."

Her lips meet the rim of her glass, but her eyes stay trained on me. I think it's the arch of her cheekbones above her hollowed cheeks that really does it for me. If her face were between my knees, maybe she'd look something like this. The intensity makes me squeeze my thighs together against a sudden kick of lust.

It's almost shocking in its strength. I used to desire Jody. I know it on a logical level, because I started sleeping with her, so of course it had to be there at some point, right? When we were young and tangled together in my narrow dorm bed, I'd been drunk on how much she wanted me, and in return it had made me so filled with lust that I'd barely been able to think.

That feeling had gone away. It's hard to tell when. I want to believe it was between moving in together and when I quit my first job at a public school. Jody pushed me into quitting, but I'd let her, and somewhere along the way she'd stopped looking at me like she wanted to strip me naked and touch me from head to toe.

It was probably earlier than that, though. Between the first argument we had and the time she'd bombed my phone with apologetic texts and voice mails. A hundred and seventy-five texts in two hours now seems creepy instead of determined.

I suck half the shot of Pappy whatever it is into my mouth. I don't care that it's expensive or rare. The fire consumes me, and I blow a breath through my teeth. "Oh my god."

"It's strong." Her teeth flash as she stifles a laugh.

"I'm going to turn into Drew Barrymore. Release the horses."

"*Firestarter?*"

"I figured it would be a better reference than that crappy Bloodhound Gang song."

She can't hide her laughter anymore. When she lets it go, she looks to the window and casts her amusement toward the beach. "What if I loved that song?"

"Do you?" Fear and embarrassment clutch my throat. "I mean, you're older than me, aren't you? Maybe it's like your high school song or something and I've stepped in it."

The dark slash of her brows quirks together in the center. "You didn't offend me so much with the song, but you're kind of doing your best now, aren't you?"

"Oh god." I cover my face for a second, but then realize I'm already holding the perfect antidote. I down the second half of my bourbon. It goes down a whole lot more smoothly than the first drink. "I'm so sorry. You're not old or anything. That's not what I meant to imply."

Hello, fishing expedition. I pretend that wasn't just incredibly awkward and keep smiling at her.

"I'm thirty-nine." Her tone is dry.

"Really?" I turn the number over in my mind, trying to get a grip on it. Is that what I would have guessed if pressed? Probably not. But she seems too mature to be in her twenties, either. Maybe that's just the feeling that she's got her life together so much more than I do. "I'm twenty-five."

I'm not where I thought I'd be at twenty-five. Maybe it's dumb, but I thought I'd have a good hold on my life by now. I'd be something closer to organized. A mile nearer to responsible.

Instead I'm living in a short-term, furnished apartment that's a favor from the parents of one of my pupils. I have a cat. At least Gyoza loves me.

I grab the fancier-looking glass and swirl the drink. "What was this one?"

"Jameson. Irish whiskey. All three of these are made the same way, just in different places. The bourbon's the American one."

I don't look up as I sip, but she's watching me steadily. "Is this less like napalm because it's a different one or because I'm getting used to it?"

"Probably because you're getting used to it. Jameson has a bit of a kick, same as the Pappy."

I take a tiny drink and let a few drops pool on my tongue. My mouth rules over my brain for a moment. This is a thing that forces me to be in the moment but soothes me at the same time. I think I like it. Maybe too much? How quickly can one become an alcoholic?

I'm being ridiculous. I swallow.

Cai chooses that moment to ask, "Does my age bother you?"

"Should it?" It's not that I'm intentionally ducking the question, but . . . I am.

"Maybe."

My gaze jerks up to hers, and I meet her head-on. "What?"

Honesty shouldn't be such a fucking shock to me. It keeps hitting me over and over again what a messed-up relationship I was in for so long. *Jody never would have* is my lament and refrain. And no, Jody never would have answered like that. "Why?"

She shrugs. "I'm fourteen years older than you. The babysitting rule."

"Are you bothered?"

"Yeah." She leans forward, resting her elbows on the table. "The thing is, I'd like to get to know you, Tansy."

My chest tightens for a moment before my heart bursts open and flutters about my rib cage. "Yeah?" *Don't be so easily pleased, Tansy. Be hard to get. Be cooler.*

"Yes." She leans forward another bit and takes a lock of my hair between her fingers. I hate that I can't feel it. I want nerves in my hair so that I don't miss any bit of this woman.

"That doesn't seem like a bad thing."

"I'm older than you, and you just got out of a long-term relationship. And I . . . I'm not looking for anything made to last forever." There's a darkness in her eyes, in the way the corners of her mouth tighten. If I asked, I'd be probing her raw spot, some old injury that doesn't look like it's ever been healed.

I don't know her story, and by the rules of every romance novel I've ever read, this is where I'm supposed to say, *It's okay, I'm only looking for a fling.* If she were Jody, I'd follow the script. I'd been trained by blasts of emotional napalm.

But I keep establishing how shitty an example my previous relationship was. So I do the exact opposite of my instincts. I stick my finger in the wound. "Why not?"

chapter

Six

TANSY

Cai's face falls. Her skin goes pale and her body language is ridiculously easy to read—she crosses both arms over her chest and even cants away from me. I haven't poked my finger in a wound—I've shoved my hand in her intestines and hauled them out onto her lap.

The urge to tell her no, it's okay, she doesn't have to say anything, hovers on my tongue, so I burn it away with more of the Jameson. I am strong. I am bold.

I tell myself so, at least.

I'd be upset with her if it seemed like she was pouting, but this isn't that. She's gone deep inside herself to consult the big book of Cai's Troubles. Sadness lurks in there. I wonder if she'll decide to tell me or not.

"It's the usual stuff. I like my life easy. I've got a lot of friends and hobbies, and I love my career. Girlfriends get upset when I pick up and leave for Alaska for a week."

So she's going with no, I guess. I could leave it be. I could.

I won't.

There's a new me, I think. I don't know why I'm this daring. Because I don't think Cai will snap off my head? Maybe because she doesn't yet know my weaknesses, the softest parts of my underbelly that bleed with a perfectly chosen jab. I have the chance to be anyone around her. Maybe I'll be someone who's not afraid of conflict.

"It sounds like you're writing a personal ad." Damn, do I like making her laugh. It makes me feel sophisticated. Smarter than I actually am, or like I'm finally one of the cool kids.

"You've got claws, kitten." She doesn't turn back toward me, but at least she uncrosses an arm and reaches toward the table.

My heart jumps when I think she's reaching for my hand, and my stomach takes the loveliest flip. But it's her bourbon she grabs. Oops. I'm such a dork sometimes. I keep my expression under control and don't betray my disappointment. Or at least I think I do.

More booze. That'll fix this pit in my gut.

I'm full of gruesome analogies tonight, I guess. The last bit of the Jameson goes down incredibly smoothly. It seems like there's now a rich umber flavor that I didn't notice before. Smoky forest stuff. Or something. "I mean, you've got a full life. None of those preclude a relationship."

"Does that mean you're looking for one with me?"

"No, I think you'd hurt me."

The words are stones tossed into a pond, with repercussions rippling out by the second. At the bar, Bonnie leans against the rail and chats with a male bartender. The floor-to-ceiling windows open at the far end of the bar are thrown open to the evening breeze. A cluster of surfers have three tables pulled together. A roar of laughter goes up from the group.

I think I recognize one of them from the covers of magazines and watch ads. He's got short-buzzed hair and eyes that are so blue I can see them from across the bar.

"That's Sean Westin." Cai's voice is quieter than usual. "He's a local."

"To San Sebastian? Or to this bar."

"Both." She reaches out, and this time she does touch my hand, covering it with hers. "I probably *would* hurt you. We shouldn't do this."

"But you agree there's something there?" Her hand is warm and her fingers are seriously skinny. I want to stroke her knuckles. I don't. "Here? Between us."

"I don't leave work in the middle of a shift for just anyone."

"I'm going to choose to believe that means you don't hit on a lot of your clients, either."

She turns her hands over and laces her fingers through mine. It's a light connection, one that makes me think about fragility and how quickly grains of sand could slide right between us. "I don't. I won't say never, but rarely."

"How long?"

"Last time was about six years ago."

I can live with that. "Is this the date you mentioned, or is it going to be some future thing?"

"Maybe both."

I don't think I can discern any differences between the Macallan and the other two I've finished, but I'm certainly starting to feel lovely. "Why would Rhett Butler drink these?"

"Because he doesn't give a damn?" I love her smile. It's inviting, like I'm being let in on a secret. "He was a guy who didn't do mixers, which means he'd also needed to drink the good stuff. That's these."

It's easy to ignore that our hands are linked together, and hard at the same time because it feels like everything centers on that connection. My rapid pulse hovers in a middle ground between anxiety and thrills. At first I hide my smile behind my glass, and then I decide that no, I'm not going to be a hiding kind of girl. Not anymore. It's okay to be happy. It's okay to be joyous. Even if this goes nowhere from here, I'm holding hands with a beautiful woman after having watched a fantastic sunset. Life is pure. Life starts again. I can start again.

I'll be damned if I let Jody take that away from me for even a second longer.

"Tell me what Idaho's like," Cai says after a long, peaceful moment.

"Cold. Insular. Filled with people who are really good people, but who only talk to each other and don't trust outsiders." I hear what I'm saying like a weird echo. It's true, but it's not all the story—but it's what Jody used to focus on when she refused to visit. I've been home only once since I've been gone. "It's beautiful though. And once people trust you, it's like joining a cult without the weird religious part."

Her laugh is a little expulsion of sound, but I like making even that come from her. "I love how you start with cold and then go into this emotional insight."

"I miss the cold." I lift my foot just enough to bring it out from under our little table. My flip-flop dangles from my painted toes. "I like these, but I used to snowshoe and ski like crazy. I used to cry every year the first day it was over sixty degrees."

"You're lying."

"Nope. Swear to god." I cross two fingers over my chest in an X. No, that isn't a petty ploy to make Cai look at my breasts . . . Okay, maybe it is, but it works. She stays smiling, but the corners of her eyes tighten and something dark passes across them. Win for me. "Mom used to call me a complete drama queen. And sure, after my cry, I'd go out to the creek with Justin and have a blast four wheeling. But I always had a cry first."

"That's fantastic."

"It's not. It's silly."

Cai shakes her head, and her hand tightens on mine. "It's adorable. You can't convince me otherwise. How did you end up here?"

"I wanted to try life in a big city. I applied to SUNY Buffalo so I could stay somewhere snowy, but USC is practically a city on its own. So that's where I ended up going." I shrug, turning my glass in circles. "I was about twelve when I figured out I was gay. The dating pool is kind of tiny in Salmon. And by tiny, I mean nonexistent."

"Seriously? No one?"

"Okay, there was Beth Karlsson. She was nice, and we gave it a shot, but we just weren't into the same stuff. Hunting's okay, but it's not my favorite."

"Wait, what?" She's laughing, and I can't tell if she's laughing at me or with me. "You've been hunting?"

"Here come the country-hick jokes." They were one of Jody's specialties. I roll my eyes in order to stave off the pinch of hurt behind my ribs.

"No way! I want to go. Can you take me?"

I freeze everything except for the way I look back up at her. "Are you teasing?"

"No." There's simplicity in her eyes that tells me she's being honest. Her mouth is curved into a slight smile. "I don't want to, like, go on a safari where I'm shooting an endangered animal in a pen or anything. But being out in the woods and part of nature and really seeing what I could do? It's an experience I haven't had."

"Are you an experience junkie?"

"Pretty much. I've already been snowboarding and skydiving and climbed mountains. I'm on the go a lot."

I'm a homebody. I can't count how many times Jody complained about my reluctance to go out with her. I didn't ever want to go shopping, or to parties, or to gallery openings. Movies hold very little appeal to me and red-carpet events even less.

But taking Cai into the woods? That's got appeal. "Ever been four wheeling?"

She shakes her head. "Driven a baja buggy in Cabo though."

"Oh, it's so much fun. Mine's at home still."

"You still consider Idaho home?"

I've never thought about it before, and suddenly I feel like a cat in a room of rocking chairs. I want to tuck in all the pieces of myself. Or better yet run and hide under a bed. "Is that bad?"

"Why would it be?" She's confused. I've confused her.

The view out the window has slipped toward evening. We've been here longer than I thought. I bite my bottom lip. "Want to go for a walk on the beach?"

She watches me for a longer moment than I'd like. She sees through me. I don't even need her to say it. "Yeah, sure."

She tosses some cash on the table, and we both wave to Bonnie. Cai also waves to the little group of surfers. A couple wave back, and one flashes a hang-loose sign. It's cute. Before I came to California, I thought people only did that in movies.

Between the stonework deck of the bar and the sandy beach is a low wall. The lack of feeling in my cheeks says maybe I've had more to drink than I thought I did, so I sit to take off my flip-flops instead of kicking them off and having to lean down. I bury my toes in the still-warm sand and a happy sigh escapes me. "Idaho doesn't have anything like this, but living in Los Feliz didn't give me much time at the beach anyway. And my new place is in San Marino. Still no beach. It's closer to school though."

"Are you getting your master's?"

"No, I'm a second-grade teacher at Woodbridge Academy."

"Never heard of it."

I shrug. "I'd be surprised if you had. It's a super tiny private school."

Cai lets her shoes dangle from two fingers and holds her free hand toward me. "Come on. Let's walk to the pier."

I squint south. The shadowy pier isn't that far away. "Okay."

I tuck my hand in Cai's as if it's perfectly natural. We have no awkward bit where we try to figure out whose hand goes in front and no one's wrist is bent at an unnatural angle. Everything as smooth as if I'd dreamed up a perfect date.

I catch the tip of my tongue between my teeth. Worry jumps on me and weighs down my shoulders. Maybe I'm living in a land of wishful thinking. It took me so long to realize that Jody was mean. It took finding her sleeping with that guy to recast everything we'd been through in a harsh light. Only then did I understand that I'd often seen what I wanted to see or swallowed lies that I wanted to hear.

Or walked away from subjects that were too hard to pursue because I was afraid of Jody's reactions.

My reactions are the ones that matter. I have to put myself first. If I can't do that, I'm bound to repeat the same mistakes over and over again.

I squeeze Cai's hand. "I understand if this is hard to talk about, but . . . I feel like there's something you're not telling me. About why you avoid commitment?"

Her sigh is easier than the snapping that I might have expected. The corners of her eyes don't tense with anger or fury. That's a good sign. "It's hard to talk about."

"I kinda figured it would be." I make my smile as endearing as I can. Except I've had three drinks, so there's a strong possibility I'm simply embarrassing myself. Normal face. Normal face. "When someone makes a blanket statement like that, that they're not looking for a relationship, one of two things are true."

"What's that?" She seems amused with me, but I'm not backing down. I don't think. I don't mean to, at least.

I tug Cai toward the water's edge. The chill of damp sand catches me first. Then the cold water is next. I let white foam roll over my toes anyway. "Either they're a full-on asshole . . ."

"I don't *think* that's me." She loops an arm around my shoulders.

We face the dark sky. There's an entire city, an entire country, an entire world at our back. It presses on me. I like the feeling, but only if I let it into me a little bit at a time. The mountains are so much safer. Maybe I should go home. "Or they have some deep dark secret."

"It's not a secret. If you google my name, you can find me." The low, dark tone of her voice sends goose bumps prickling across my arms. I want to take my questions back at the same time that I'm desperate to know her truths. "I did some interviews. 'We're looking for Xue. We love her. Please let her come home.'"

My voice is a whisper. "Who's Xue?"

"Was." She finally looks at me. There are shadows across her face. The beach is dark and we're in the dark together, but I still don't think she sees me. Not really. "She was my older sister."

"What happened to her?" I lean into her, my shoulder against her side. I wish I could say I was holding her up, but I'm not. She stands all on her own.

"She was in college and walking away from campus. Abducted. Missing for more than seven months." She sighs, a long and deep sound that's filled with a whole family's pain and anguish. "At least we eventually got to have a funeral."

"Oh god," I breathe. "I'm so sorry. For you, for your family. When was it?"

"High school." She starts walking toward the pier again, slowly enough that I feel okay walking next to her. She's not trying to get away. "I spent most of my freshman year searching the desert, hoping I wasn't the one to find my sister's body."

chapter

Seven

CAI

The terror is sudden and fresh, as if it hasn't been twenty-five years and as if I haven't been to three different therapists to deal with issues that cropped up throughout my life. I taste copper and my bitter fear. When I swallow them, I nearly puke.

I can't believe I said that part of it. That my sister died, that it was a terrible experience, that we eventually had to bury her—all that I've told before. But I have never breathed a word of my fear at coming across a sun-bleached skull and knowing with my deep soul that it was Xue. It wasn't anyone's business but mine, and here I am spilling everything to this woman I barely know.

Maybe that's it. Maybe it's the fact that I hardly know more than her name, but I've seen her completely undone and still made of resiliency. Most people wouldn't have been able to gather their thoughts and their sense of self the way Tansy had on her wedding day. I'm astonished by her continuing bravery.

"This way," I mutter, and break to head toward the pier like I had originally planned.

Tansy follows me. I guess I didn't expect that, because my surprise is a live animal that throat-punches my fear and takes its place. I'm not sure what I expected. That she would run away screaming? It'll be an easier, quieter thing than that. We'll have a couple of phone calls and maybe text a couple of times, and then she'll just disappear. Another ghost in my life. I have so many, I could start a haunted house.

"How old were you?"

The wind snatches her voice away so that I barely hear her. It's more than enough, though. "Fourteen."

"I'm sorry."

My feet drag me to a stop, almost against my will.

Tansy's hair is blowing in the breeze. With the light gone, I can't see the color of the curl she pulls away from her mouth. I know that orange-red, though. I think I'll see it in my dreams for a very, very long time. "You weren't there."

"Believe it or not, that's part of what I'm sorry for. I think maybe you were really alone."

I shake my head. "I had all my family with me. Cousins, aunts. Three out of four grandparents. My mom and dad."

"Not that kind of alone."

"What other kind is there?"

We're standing close. Toe to toe nearly, and it wouldn't take much to put my hand on the waist of her jean shorts, under the open flannel shirt. Her gaze searches my face. I don't know what she's looking for.

I'm not sure if I want her to find it.

She lifts a single finger, lays it on my chest, just left of my sternum. "Alone in here. When you don't have anyone with you."

"You know how that feels?"

"I do. I've been alone when I was with someone who was supposed to love me. Supposed to cherish me. And she didn't."

Her mouth is a perfect bow. I cup the side of her face and scrub my thumb over her bottom lip. She lets me. In the dark, I see only the lighter shadow of her bottom teeth. "My family loves me."

"But did you trust them? Probably you did before and maybe you did afterward, but when you were walking through that desert? Looking. Hoping to find her and scared to death of finding her." She slowly shakes her head. "You didn't tell anyone that."

"How do you know?"

"Because I didn't tell anyone when I was so hopeless either."

I kiss her. I want to, but I don't mean to, and still I take her mouth before I can think it through. What kind of fucked-up nonseduction conversation is this? But then her hands fist in my tank top and little, delicate Tansy drags me closer to her at the same time that her mouth melts under mine. I lick into her, tasting the last dregs of sharp whiskey on her tongue. Taking it for my own.

I fold one hand against the small of her back where she's surprisingly lithe. Muscles shift under my touch as she moves closer to me. I gather her lips and tongue and teeth, and I don't let her go. This is new. We're new. I can't tell if I'm catching a wave or being shoved under.

I like her hands curled around my shirt, but I like the way her thumbs rub up and down my skin even more. I catch my breath and let it free between her lips.

"We can't do this," I say against her mouth.

Even as I say it, I notice how I'm pulling her closer and closer, until her breasts are brushing mine. Too many damn shirts and layers. I want to feel her tight nipples against me.

"Probably not." She breaks her mouth free, and for a shuddering heartbeat I think she's going to free herself completely. Instead she opens her mouth against my neck.

On instinct, I wrap a hand in her curls and yank. She hisses in a gasp and her eyes glimmer under lowered lashes. "Do you play like that?"

"Do you?"

"No," she says and the answer surprises me. Until she tries to lower her head against the grip I still have on her at the same time that she presses her hips against me. "But I wanted to. Jody—" She cuts herself off.

"You can say it."

"Jody said S&M was for desperate losers. Straight people pretending their lives could still be exciting."

"Jody sounds like a cunt."

She squeaks with laughter that breaks the mood and yet lets it build at the same time. "I guess she was. Is. I don't know."

"Is. Definitely currently." I gentle my hold on her hair, but the strands are still twined around my fingers.

"I think you're right. I'm lucky enough that I don't have to deal with her anymore."

"You were right," I admit. "I closed my family out for a long time. Went away to school on the East Coast for a couple years, before

I dropped out. I still have distance, since they live down in San Diego. It's never going to be the way it was, but it's better now."

"I'm glad."

"I like your smile."

It grows wide enough that I can see her dimples in the dark. "I'm glad for that too."

I start walking again, but this time I take her hand in mine. Our palms are matched. My fingers are a little bit longer than hers, but not by much. I hold one of her hands between both of mine, tracing the structure of her knuckles. Besotted swain and all that happy crappy, I guess, but I'm kind of loopy. This girl is special.

Shit, or maybe I just want her to be special. I want a way outside my own head, someone to inspire a grand romance. I wasn't playing earlier. Long-term relationships don't happen to me or with me, and I didn't mentioned this part, but I've been wondering for a while if it's some kind of failing of mine. I'm too pragmatic to be passionate enough. Orgasms are orgasms and movie-watching buddies are great and someone to go to dinner with is wonderful. But there's never been anyone I couldn't live without after that initial flush of addiction and mesmerism.

It never takes long before the magic wears off.

And I wonder if maybe I'll break this girl's heart without trying too hard.

The pier is quiet after dark. Where pier meets sidewalk, there's a business that rents bikes and Segways during the daytime. The ice cream stand and bait shop at the end close at dusk. Ninety percent of the tourists and all the surfers have gone home to rest up for another day of chasing skin cancer tomorrow.

"I don't come out here much during the day," I say. We're on the firm, wet sand closest to the water. A rogue wave sometimes chases all the way up to our toes.

"Not into swimming?"

"Not really. Or having all my tattoos fade just because I don't take care of them."

Tansy pushes hair away from her neck. She's looking out at the water, not at me. "The ocean is scary. Sometimes I want to go home to the mountains."

"There's mountains in California."

She shrugs. "I guess you could call them that. Sort of dinky compared to what I'm used to." I barely hear her sigh. "Or was used to. It's been a long time since I've been home."

"How long?"

"Four years." She glances back at me, looking over her shoulder. "That's too long to go without visiting your family, isn't it?"

"I think my mom would probably show up on my doorstep and bang on the door until I let her in after about four months." My family is intrusive and nosy and I can't imagine my life without them. "Why has it been so long? Did you have a fight?"

"No. I mean, I've seen them. Mom and Dad have come to visit twice and my brother came when he graduated college. But I haven't been to Idaho. It's because of my ex. She wasn't fond of anywhere that could remotely be called a flyover state."

I smooth her hair back from her face. The strands are more wiry than they look, but I love her hair. It's practically alive. "Couldn't you go without her?"

Her laugh is wry and only a little bitter. "There's no going anywhere without Jody. She'll be unendurable for weeks."

"There was."

"What?"

"There *was* no going anywhere without her. You're free now." The skin at the joint between her cheek and ear is incredibly soft under my thumb. I've touched plenty of girls in my life, but I swear she's softer than any of them.

And when her smile blooms, it's so beautiful that I can feel its beauty in my chest. "You're right. Man, that's a nice thought. Thank you for that."

"I didn't do it. You did, by walking away from your wedding."

"It wasn't quite as easy as that." Her smile dims a little. "It wasn't all done that day. But thanks for the reminder, then."

"I like to be useful," I tease.

"Excellent personality trait. It might make up for the fact that it kinda feels like you're taking me somewhere murdery."

"Murdery?" I die laughing. "What?"

She waves toward the even deeper shadows under the pier. "You seem to be heading under the pier? I'm not going under there, you realize that, right? I don't mean to offend you, but I'd be really, really upset to be killed tonight."

"Oh god, I'm sorry." I lift both hands, showing her my palms and trying not to laugh so hard that she thinks I'm dismissing her. "Yeah, I was headed there—it's a place I like to go when I want some peace and quiet. The waves sound really cool. But we totally don't have to. I understand, I promise."

"Good." She tugs my hand toward the sidewalk and the lights of stores and cafés. San Sebastian is pretty quiet at night. "I think in a TV show, this is where I'd be all 'No, since you're willing to back down, we can go,' but . . . still not going. Glad you're responding well though."

"I'm sorry. My danger radar is a little warped." I make myself shrug. "It's a side effect, I guess. My friend Brooke's nickname for me is Recky."

"Recky?"

"As in reckless."

We pull to a stop on the sidewalk. Across the street begins the main drag of San Sebastian. I hear distant chatter and a note or two of saxophone from a sidewalk musician. It's a nice place to hang out. Behind us is the steady roar of the ocean.

I want to stay here with Tansy in the quiet between two worlds.

I cup her face in my hands. "I'm sorry I scared you."

"I'm sorry if I overreacted."

"It's fine. I'll take you back one day when it's sunny and there's people around."

"Who can hear me scream if you try to stab me," she says, but there's a happy lilt in her voice.

"I solemnly swear not to stab, maim, or strangle you."

Her head tilts. Her cloud of hair pours over my wrist with a tickle. "Does *maim* belong in that trio? I feel like it's not up to snuff."

I narrow my eyes, studying her. "Was that a pun?"

Her expression goes so open and wide and innocent that I know she's having me on. "Only a monster would make a pun about snuff films."

"Maybe you're the one I have to watch out for."

"Maybe," she echoes.

This girl is joy. So much younger than me. She's like a kitten who needs to be wrapped in a blanket burrito—and then she goes and makes a joke about death films. I'm not entirely sure what to do about her.

So I kiss her. That way neither of us has to think.

And, damn, is that a good decision.

chapter

Eight

TANSY

"No, Edgar, we don't lick paint off our fingers. That's not organic." I snag Edgar's wrists in one hand and wipe pastel pink off both his palms.

"Sorry," he says. His smile is missing his two front teeth. "Do you like my picture?"

I clothespin it to the drying cord that stretches above my head. "It's lovely. Is it going to be a present for your mommy?"

"No, probably for Daddy's new girlfriend. She's nice, but he says that she's only one of his temporary—" His missing teeth turn the *t* into a *th*, and he stumbles over the rest of the word. "Daddy's friend for a little bit. So I wanted to make her a picture for when she goes away."

Good lord. I squeeze Edgar's narrow shoulder. He's a sweet boy with a propensity for saying exactly what's on his mind. I wonder if his dad, an insanely successful record producer, has any idea what gets out to the rest of the world. If I sold this story to a tabloid, I'd have a fat check. Not that it would be enough to counter being sued within an inch of my life for violating my nondisclosure agreements.

Of course, that's part of why I make such a fantastic salary. I'm paid for my discretion as much as for my skills.

I place a finger over my lips and lift another in the air as I circle the room. All five of my students rush to the Swedish hand-knotted rya rug and sit. Edgar leans his head on Stella's shoulder. I'd say something about it, but she's playing with his longish brown hair, winding it around a finger, so I don't think she minds. "Who wants to lead our end-of-day discussion?"

"Me! Me!" Corbyn bounces on her knees with one hand in the air.

"You went yesterday, Corbyn."

She looks around. None of their little faces look ready to challenge her. "They don't mind."

I gentle my voice. "We were going to work on letting others vocalize their feelings, remember, Corbyn?"

She blinks at me. Her lashes are long, framing unnaturally green eyes. They're the kind of color I would suspect to be contacts in a grown-up, but I've seen her mother. Millions of Americans have seen her movies too. The eyes are real. She turns to Mink, sitting beside her with his legs crossed. He has both hands twisted in the carpet's long tufts. "Mink, tell me you don't mind."

Mink is a quiet little boy. I think he might have a crush on Edgar. It's hard to navigate such a small classroom sometimes. "I don't mind," he whispers.

I hold in my sigh and let Corbyn proceed with our after-action review. She starts with the top three lessons learned from the day before moving on to her favorite part: praise and promotion. "And I did the best with my penmanship."

"No one does 'the best.' You experienced your full potential."

"Mink did good too," she throws out by way of making up. She bestows a smile on the boy. She's sure lucky she takes after her mother and not her awkward and knobby musician father.

"Mink did well," I say, correcting her grammar. "Stella, why don't you tell us a little something about your time with Madame Pillet?"

"*Le début de la nouvelle année scolaire me lasse.*"

"Well done!" Each of the children go in pairs for their French lessons. I clap. I don't actually know what she's saying—I took Spanish. "Madame Pillet said you are learning very quickly."

Her cheeks turn pink, but she doesn't look away. It's a vast improvement on the nearly mute girl who'd first joined our class mid last year. "Thank you, Ms. Gavin."

"Thank you for your efforts."

We wrap up a few more things, and then I help them gather their bags. Edgar has a Transformers backpack. Corbyn's bag was hand sewn in Tibet. Stella puts her notebooks in a purple Hermes messenger bag.

My job is so weird sometimes. As Jody used to tell me, there are a thousand teachers in Southern California who'd kill for this job. I'm lucky as heck, but I don't know if I'm right for it. I'm not meant for this tiny world of privilege.

I walk the kids to the courtyard. The semicircle is paved in red stone that blends in with the water-conscious semi-arid design of the front gardens. The long line of Lexuses and Mercedes and Teslas kind of stands out a little bit, however.

I wave to Imogene, the fifth-grade teacher who's as close to what I can call a friend at the school. She has Wren Baccus by the hand, and she rolls her eyes subtly, then tips her chin down at the eleven-year-old, who's wearing a T-shirt with a kitten dressed as a knight, riding a llama. Good lord, what could that child have done now?

The first car that pulls up to my small pod is a convertible Rolls-Royce. Mrs. Dousseau has the top down. One of our school aides-de-camp ushers Mink into the back seat and begins buckling him into his leather-lined booster seat.

"Good afternoon, Therese. Mink has a particularly challenging logic puzzle this evening. We're evaluating expressions with variables."

She has one hand draped on the steering wheel and the other resting on the stick shift. Her outfit is immaculately put together. Even though on one level you could call it a simple athleisure set, it's not. Not with the way her legs look in those leggings and not with the artfully casual drape of the tank top over her strappy sports bra. And the cleavage. Jesus Christ, she has gorgeous cleavage.

Even with the butterflies I get thinking about Cai, I can still appreciate Mrs. Dousseau's ample bounty. She's a trophy wife of the highest caste. It would be insensitive to ignore her perfection.

It helps that she's nice. "Thank you, Tansy. You help him achieve so much. Are there instructions?"

"Of course." I handwrite carefully crafted parent guidelines for everything that goes home with my kids. It's the personal touch that our academy strives for. It's also another piece of why I make my nice salary. "They're in his folder."

"I think Meredith will have a nice snack waiting for us, and then we'll settle in to work on it together." She catches Mink's eye in the rearview mirror. "How does a berry bowl sound, sweetheart?"

"With whipped cream?" His hair slides into his eyes.

"Most certainly," she assures him.

I'm guessing he doesn't mean the type that comes in a metal can and not the kind in a tub, either. Meredith is in an airy kitchen with travertine counters holding a bowl and a whisk at this very moment.

"Great," he says in his little voice.

"Have a nice afternoon, Mink. Mrs. Dousseau." I step back and wave as they drive away.

One down, four more to go. It's not my favorite part of the day. The parents who send their children to Woodbridge Academy are the kind who thrive on personal attention. I'm expected to interact with them as if I wouldn't wish to be anywhere else. I'm able to go more quickly with Stella's ride, as the nanny is way more interested in getting on with her day than in chitchat.

And then my children have all been sent off and I'm alone in the courtyard except for a couple of other teachers. Imogene waves me down.

"What happened?" I ask, ready for a good one.

"I'm fat." She says it deadpan, which makes it all the funnier because when she's holding her mouth flat, her cheekbones are stupidly sharp and high. Her skin is a dark, rich brown and her hair is trimmed into a teeny-weeny afro that emphasizes the starkness of her features.

I gasp and laugh at the same time. "What in the world?"

"I had both butternut squash and feta on my salad." She lifts her eyebrows. "Wren thinks I should have picked either one or the other, and skipped the dressing too. Since she's looking out for me, with that twenty pounds I should lose and all."

"Oh that sweet baby angel." I'm torn between laughing and dying of worry. "You know she's got to be hearing that at home."

Imogene sighs. "I know. Best-case scenario, she's hearing her mom talk. Worst-case, someone's nitpicking her food like that."

"We might want to pop into Teddy's office and let him know."

She loops her arm through mine. "Does Wren need the psych eval or do I?"

"I think we all do for working here," I tease. I have my hair twisted up on my head, so the sun feels good on the back of my neck. "You doubly do if you believe Wren that you're overweight. If you lost twenty, you'd be ill."

"You're such a sweetheart. But if we're going to the administration building, we absolutely have to swing by the front desk."

"Why?" A little knot appears between my brows. I rub it with two fingers. "What's going on?"

"I stopped in earlier and saw something special." By the last two words, she's using a singsong voice.

"What is it?" My heart and stomach switch places.

Obviously everyone knows that I walked out on the wedding. I tried not to make a big deal about it, but I came back to school without a wedding ring and without even an engagement ring. No pictures of a tropical honeymoon either. People didn't really make a fuss. I've always kept my relationship private. I used to think I did it because I was a private person, but lately I've started to realize it's because part of me knew if I talked about what Jody said to me, everyone would know how wrong things were.

Imogene was thrilled that I'd finally be able to join "the girls" for drinks a week after school started. I felt awkward in my usual way, but I made it through. It had been easier knowing there was no one at home stewing in their upset, preparing to ice me out with three days of silent treatment.

But no one understood what my breakup with Jody had really been like. What it had done to me.

We live in a world where bad things happen in the dark. But we also live in a world where bad things can happen in the daytime and look absolutely normal to the people around us.

Imogene shook her head. "I'm not going to be the one to ruin the surprise."

I swallow and try to act like this is normal. Like everything's going to be fine.

The administration building is at the back of our twelve-acre campus. It doesn't seem that large until I remember all over again that it's nestled between Beverly Hills properties and land is at a premium. The three-thousand-square-foot Craftsman cottage is the original house built for a movie producer in 1917. It was his son who started the academy in the late forties in order to service the children of movie stars who wanted an environment that guaranteed privacy.

The pitched, single-clad roof casts shadows over us before we even climb the porch. I shiver. My mind can't even come up with what I'm fearing—all I know is that my dread is wrapped up in Jody.

Imogene rubs my arm. "Everything okay?"

"Sure, yeah." I manage to smile. "Caught a chill. What's the old saying? 'A goose walked over my grave'?"

"My grandmamma used to say that. She also used to say 'Don't kid a kidder.'" She stops with one hand on the brass knob of the front door.

I can't see the front office through the leaded glass. I don't know what's waiting for me. I'm not okay with doing this right now. "I don't know what you're talking about."

"When I was seventeen, I had a boyfriend who liked to pick my outfits. It was cute. At first. But then he started talking about how maybe I should throw out the things that he didn't like since it wasn't like I needed that trashy stuff anyways. I did it."

My gaze jumps to hers. I can't say anything. My throat is filled with bees.

"Things got worse from there." She looks away from me and to the flawless tennis courts next to the admin building. "They got better eventually, but . . . if you need to talk to anyone, I'm here."

What I'm supposed to feel is gratitude. As if the arms of friendship have been opened to me. But I'm consumed by all-encompassing anger. "Why didn't you say anything?"

"I didn't want to make assumptions." Her eyes are dark brown and filled with a kind of pity that makes me sick. "I wasn't sure if you'd listen to me anyway."

Instead she let me stay in an unhealthy relationship. She let me become smaller. I know staying with Jody was my fault. I made my own choices. But I can't help but wonder if things would have been different if I'd had friends who were willing to speak up. I don't know how much of that is my fault and how much is living in Southern

California where no one really knows anyone and how much was Jody making sure that I didn't have friends.

My chest clenches, and my eyes go wide enough that I must be giving that girl on *Orange Is the New Black* a run for her money. Crazy Eyes 2.0, that's me. "Does everyone on staff know? Did they? Do people talk about me?"

She shakes her head, but I see the way her mouth twists before she can assemble it into calming reassurance. "Gossip sucks."

I'm a walking wound, made of vulnerability and flayed open. "Sure."

At least I'm not scared of the mysterious surprise awaiting me at the front desk anymore. I could practically laugh, except I hold it in because I'm thinking adding hysteria to all this is not so good. Not so great at all.

I'm shaking my head as I go inside, because my other option is probably screaming. I'm made of *probably* and *maybe*. I can't think my way through anything right now. "Hi, Tracy."

Tracy Macnamara, the academy's receptionist, looks up from her computer and waves. "Hi, Tansy."

I don't see any roses or obvious bouquets waiting for me. The main office looks like a cozy living room that just happens to have Tracy's desk in the northern corner under a window framed by hand-painted wainscoting. No curtains are necessary since the deep profile of the Craftsman-style roof shades all the windows. Deep wing chairs upholstered in worn brown leather frame both sides of the fireplace.

Even Tracy's desk is bare but for her MacBook Air and the phone console she controls as brusquely as one of those old-school telephone exchange operators. She points to the open archway beside her with her usual nearly psychic sense of what people need. "In the kitchen."

"Thanks."

The kitchen is as striking as the rest of the house. The subway-style tile is cream and green, with more of the bright-green splashed above the counters. Since it's used as an occasional classroom and to prepare food for staff meetings, everything is top of the line and commercial grade.

Sitting next to the eight-burner Vulcan range is a basket wrapped in pale-green cellophane. Instantly I know that Jody had nothing to do with it. The painted basket is too quirky and filled with a pile of cat toys. Jody always hated Gyoza. This has Cai's name all over it. "Is this it?"

"Yeah," Imogene confirms. "It was on Tracy's desk, but you know how she is. Can't stand even a Post-it Note. What's in it? Are those sex toys?"

I flare red-hot, and it's an indescribable combination of embarrassment and pure turn-on. I wonder what it would be like to get there with Cai. To feel her hands on me and her mouth on me and her attention on me. I shiver. "No, I think they're cat toys."

From across the spacious room, the black sticks with feathers looked a little like ticklers, but they're cat teasers. I run pink feathers through my fingers. There are also toy mice and a catnip toy and some treats in a cellophane bag. "Gyoza is going to love these."

"Somebody definitely knows you're a crazy cat lady."

"It seems like it."

I hate to keep comparing Cai to Jody, but isn't it okay if it's always in her favor? She thought of and found something that's really me, just from a few minutes of me talking about my cat. Jody . . . Jody's go-to was red roses. I hated to complain, because she'd get so hurt and tell me I never appreciated anything. She'd swing back the other way then. It hurt when she didn't talk to me for days.

"Is there a card?" Imogene pokes a fluffy knot of fleece.

I don't growl. I don't smack her hand away territorially. Points to me for being a grown-up? I guess. I pick up the whole basket instead, as if I'm turning it to look for the card. Really, I just want to keep it all to myself. It's my perfect present. My thing that makes my chest warm and my heart happy in a way that, oh crap, is also bringing tears to my eyes. "No card."

"But you know who they're from?"

"Yeah."

"Is it Stella's parents? Do they want you to babysit again?"

God, why wasn't she this nosy when I was stuck with Jody? "No, it's personal. I'm just going to take this to my car. I'll catch you later, okay?"

"Let's get brunch this weekend," she calls as I leave the room.

I wave. "Sounds good. I'll call you."

And isn't that a weird feeling? I'm free to call her—or not call her—as I like. It's all my choice. I don't have to worry about whether anyone in my life will mind if I go out for pancakes and leave them alone, or if I don't make them breakfast.

I'm free. I have my own life to build.

I put the basket in the back seat and lean against my sun-warmed car. Too impatient to even get in, I fish my phone out of my pocket.

Tansy: *Thanks.*

Cai: *:) You like?*

Tansy: *I do. And Gyoza will like it all even more. How can I thank you?*

Cai: *Dinner?*

Tansy: *Sure. Want me to bring something to the tattoo shop? What do you want me to cook?*

Cai: *No, you and me going out.*

My heart, the one that had felt so soft and gooey moments ago, leaps up to my throat and chokes me. I'm an idiot. I'm such a fucking idiot. The way my hands start to shake makes it hard to type my response. *Sure. Tell me when & where.*

She answers with the name of a restaurant and a time, but I'm already stuck in a shame spiral. Of course she meant going out together. That's what normal people do. I jumped immediately to the most subservient, abnormal reaction.

She's going to be so annoyed with me.

chapter

Nine

CAI

I love first dates. And yeah, maybe the time we spent together at Mikey's and on the beach was supposed to count as a first, but waiting for Tansy outside the bistro I've picked has the feel of one. Plus I did official, actual asking this time. That's always a cool milestone.

Watching Tansy walk up to me is a treat. She's wearing a skirt, a fluttery thing that skims around her ankles with fat purple slashes of color. The top is peasant style, with a straight across neckline that does crazy shit to my self-control. I want to touch her. It wouldn't take much. A hand on that pale, milky skin would be enough.

My fingers curl in over my palms.

Her hair falls down her back in a riotous mass of curls. The smile she gives me is tentative, and she shoves a piece of hair behind her ear as she looks up at me from under her lashes. "Hi."

There's tension in her neck that pulls the strings of her tendons taut. "Hi."

We stand there for a moment, another breath, another handful of seconds as cars whoosh by in the street. "We should head in."

Except I reach out to take her hand and she flinches—a little step backward and the jolt of her chin that she tries to hide by looking down the street. "I'm sorry about yesterday. When I thought you wanted . . ."

I try to give her the space she needs to gather her words, but she seems to only dig herself deeper. Her mouth opens, and she looks back at me—and then away again.

"About bringing food? It's not a big deal. Do you like to cook?"

"No, I mean, yes."

"It's okay to not like cooking. That's why restaurants exist." I point at the place beside us, trying to be cheeky. There's a big chunk of this puzzle that I'm not understanding, especially when she looks at me with tragically big eyes.

I shove my hands in the pockets of my pinstriped trousers, purposely hiding them so she'll feel better and maybe less flinchy. I hate being out of my element. I hate the way I'm looking at her as if she's a bomb that's going to go off, but I can't help it either. This is the stuff that I'm so bad with. It wrecks me to see her like this, and for Christ's sake all I said was something totally normal.

"I'm domestic. I like baking and decorating."

I let my head cock. "Those are not the same thing as cooking. They're, like, different sections in home ec and everything."

"I know that." She tries to smile at me, and god, I can't take it anymore.

"Come here." I reach out, slowly this time so she doesn't jump.

I take her shoulders and pull her to me. She's stiff as fuck, but she doesn't seem exactly unwilling. More like unsure of where to put her face. I cup the back of her head and nudge her toward my shoulder.

And, the second her cheek touches me, she bursts into tears.

Fuck. Hell. I beat back the panic. This is fine. I know what I'm doing. I can be here for her enough that I won't let her crash and burn. "What's wrong?"

"You're so nice." Her words fight their way free from between whimpering sobs. She puts a hand over her eyes, shoves away the tears spilling over her cheeks again and again.

"That's not normally a cry-worthy thing."

"See? Even in this?" She sniffles. "I'm a mess. You should get away from me."

"Do you want me to?" I'm such a shitty person, because part of me wants her to say yes and let me off the hook. It's a small part, but it's still there at the scared center of my chest. Tansy wouldn't have this small selfish bit—her courage wouldn't allow her to. Even her tears are wide open. I don't think I've met anyone exactly like her before.

She doesn't answer in words. One hand clutches the placket of my button-down shirt, while the other slips around my waist. She burrows against me like a kitten. Needy and helpless. Her whole body shakes with her crying.

She's easy to take care of. Most of me is ready to stand here on this corner until the world burns away as long as that's what she needs. I rub her narrow back. Her curls tickle my hand.

I avoid her bare shoulders because it's the right thing to do. The hard thing, but the right thing, and if I'm admitting to myself that a little bit wants to run, then the least I can do is be a decent human with the rest of me.

Eventually she subsides. Her sniffles clear her nose. She wipes her cheeks clean and pulls back only enough to look at me. Her eyes are glassy, and her nose pink at the rim. That's being kind. She's as red as Rudolph. It's kind of adorable. "I don't know what's wrong with me. I'm not a crier."

"People have emotions. It's chill."

"It's such a girl thing." Her words break in the middle, and she hides her face against me again.

"So?"

She freezes. Every bit of her. I don't think even a curl moves. She scrubs her nose with the base of her palm. "What?"

"So what if it's a girl thing?" A seam runs down the middle of her shirt. I trace the material with a finger. She arches into my touch just a little bit. "I mean, you're a girl, right? I kind of hope so, since I'm a lesbian and I find you remarkably attractive."

My teasing works. A smile lifts her mouth. "I'm a girl. And you're a goofball."

"Sometimes." I run my thumb over the curve of her cheek, which is tacky with drying tears and hot with the force of her emotion. "Are you hungry?"

"Not really."

"Then do you mind if we get out of here? Trust me enough to take a ride with me?"

"I'm sorry if I'm overly cautious. I watch way too many shows with names like *Snapped* and *Swamp Murders*."

I'm taken aback for a second, enough that I duck my knees the inches needed to look her in the eyes. "There's enough killings in swamps that they can have a whole show about them?"

She pushes her hair back from her face. A breeze catches the hem of her dress and wraps it around both our calves. "People vastly underestimate the number of swamps in America. Michigan has swamps. Wisconsin. They're all over."

"Still, I feel like the vast majority of that show has to take place in Louisiana. It's probably contractual or something."

"I'll ride in your car."

"And if I say I've actually got a motorcycle?"

Her eyes light up. Her smile gets so big it almost seems to lift her off her toes. "Seriously?"

"It gets great gas mileage."

"As if that's the only reason you got it." She wrinkles her nose when she scoffs.

"You know my name, not my story." I'm jokes right and left around this girl. It's almost weird how much I want her to smile.

It's good when she giggles. There's a force that's right with the world. I take her hand and the feeling only gets stronger.

"I can't." She gestures to her long skirt. "It'd be in the way, wouldn't it? Like a cape near a propeller? 'No capes!'"

An *Incredibles* references. Be still my poor heart. "We can work around it if you're not afraid to show a little leg."

She flashes me a saucy grin. "I like my legs." But just as quickly the smile is gone. She's thinking of her ex. I know it without asking. That's what all of this is. Jody was a bitch and Tansy is a broken girl.

I'm not a doctor. I don't repair broken people. I should run.

My bike is up the street in a parking garage. The shadowy recesses make the enamel and black pipes look pretty damn impressive. I pat the fender. "This is my baby. She's on the smaller side, but she's a hard as hell worker."

"Is it a Harley? It looks like one but not at the same time." She trails a hand over the black leather seat. "I don't think I've seen a red Harley before."

"It's a Victory Vegas." I pet the painted frame. "I love my baby. The price for performance can't be beat. I got it last year, but I've had plenty of bikes in my life. You can trust me."

She looks up at me with wide eyes and a soft bend to her lower lip that isn't quite smile, isn't quite sadness. "I do. Maybe I shouldn't yet, but I do."

I hand her my extra helmet, and I have to teach her how to tie up her skirt, get on, and put her arms around my waist. I gave her a quick rundown on how to lean into curves. I like the way her grip tightens when I kick the engine on. "You ready?"

"Probably not," she says, and then she giggles. She presses her face against my back. "Okay, let's do this."

I take it slow at first. She falls into the pattern easily, moving with me. Her thighs are initially tense, but by the time I navigate us toward the Pacific Coast Highway, she's snuggled up against me. It takes another twenty minutes of cruising before she's okay enough to lift her head from my shoulder.

There's traffic, so it's not as if we're going fast. I'm glad I installed the passenger seat today. I don't always.

At a light, she's brave enough to let go of my waist and stretch her arms to the side. "This feels so weird. I'm supposed to be protected by a box."

"Weird in a good way?"

"Definitely." The light turns green, and she holds on to me again. "Definitely a good way."

I don't have a direction in mind at first, but I'm driving north, so it doesn't take me long to think of where to go. It's in Long Beach, but traffic is kind to us, and we make good time in the scheme of California gridlock.

"What's this?" Tansy asks as she stands beside my bike in the parking lot. Once she takes off the helmet, she shakes out her hair, fluffing and squishing it without ever actually running her hands through the curls. "Aquarium of the Pacific? Do they have otters? I love otters and manatees."

"Somehow that doesn't surprise me." I take her hand and pull her closer to me, close enough that I can smell her sweet perfume mixing with the saltiness that's her skin.

"Sea cows have a pretty sweet life. They cruise around and munch veggies all day. I could live like that. Sounds pretty low stress."

"I'd miss Netflix."

"I'm a Hulu girl. We're doomed." She rests her head on my shoulder as we approach the entrance.

"It depends. One more thing might save us or break us: HBO Go or Starz?"

"Ugh, HBO all the way. I'd die without *Westworld*."

"Life is still worth living."

She laughs and I kiss her. Fast and quick, but enough to take the taste of her happiness into myself. It's hard to believe that only an hour ago she was sobbing in my arms on a city street. "You're beautiful when you laugh," I tell her.

She gasps, a tiny expulsion of noise.

"Hasn't anyone told you that?"

She shakes her head. Her hand tightens on mine. "I like it though."

I cup the side of her face, and I almost say something more, something that I'd probably regret later when my ghosts catch up to me and I fuck all this up. I shove away all the could-have-beens and should-says. "Let's go in."

We're the only ones at the ticket window. "Are you sure," Tansy asks, squeezing my hand. "It closes in an hour."

"That's enough time for what I'm thinking about."

"Is that supposed to sound as naughty as it does?" She's teasing, but she's reaching pretty hard for the joke. She's trying to be whatever kind of normal, whatever sort of person she thinks I want her to be.

I want her to be her. Campsite rules and all that. I'm older than her. If I'm willing to do this with Tansy, I have to be able to leave her better off than I found her. That seems easier said than done when I'm pretty much a hot mess at any given time. I laugh, but say, "Not intentionally. Nothing's naughty when there's birds involved."

"Birds?" She trails along behind me, but I can practically picture the confused line between her brows. "We're at an aquarium. Did you get lost?"

"Nope. We're almost there."

You can hear the lorikeet enclosure before you turn the corner and see the giant cage. They cover it over with as much vegetation as possible, but there's still no denying the honeycombed metal fencing. There's a door that's practically an airlock and then a small counter, where I pay for two cups of nectar. Hanging plastic hides the inside of the enclosure from view until I push them aside. "Welcome to heaven."

chapter

Ten

TANSY

I step into the middle of the path and turn in a slow circle. We've entered a jungle. Sure, it's covered overhead and with wooden rail fences along the path, but somehow . . . somehow I don't care about that. Even though it's the opposite end of the spectrum from the soaring trees and mountain creeks of Idaho, it feels a little like home. It's the chance to trade buildings and concrete for nature. My breath flutters, and I grin so hard my cheeks hurt. "The birds are *everywhere.*"

"Here, hold your cup like this." Cai guides my hand so that I'm holding the nectar as if I'm making a horizontal okay sign.

It's only a moment before a green bird with a bright-red chest lands on my wrist. I squeal a little. It hops but doesn't fly away. Instead it leans down and licks up some of the juice. "Holy cannoli!"

I love her laugh. It's full and rich in a way that sets my skin tingling. "Did you really just say that?"

"No?" I try, even though it's a blatant lie.

"You don't curse? Ever?"

"I work with little kids who are old enough to know what the 'bad' words are. If I slip, they take huge pleasure in acting incredibly scandalized. And then they run home and tell their parents. So I avoid the problem by not getting in the habit."

And here I pause, waiting for the negative reaction that I'm so, so used to. It's like waiting for the shoe to drop, and honestly, the fact that it's not coming makes me kind of more anxious than ever.

Like maybe it's just building up steam and going to come down on me like a ton of bricks. My brain is so spinny that I can't even keep my metaphors straight.

I focus on the bird, who's taken over my wrist as if I was made to be its perch.

"We're so opposite, it's kind of ridiculous," Cai says. "Half the time I feel like I have to practice cussing more so I fit into people's expectations of a tattoo artist."

I shouldn't be surprised by Cai's depths by now. But it's a weirdly soothing circle. I want the unexpected since I always expect terribleness. "Maybe that means we meet in the middle."

Her smile is huge. Not only the outside of her eyes crinkle, the inside corner does too. I step closer because I can't help it. I'm caught in her orbit, and I like it here. She steps toward me too, but instead of touching me, she only holds her cup of syrup next to mine.

The motion is enough to catch the attention of more birds. One lands on Cai, then another lights on my shoulder. I giggle instead of squeal this time. Still completely childish, but I don't care. I don't feel that heavy stare that means I'd have to explain myself later.

The bird is dainty, but there's no mistaking the pinch as it holds on. Another lands on me, shoving in between my neck and its friend. "Oh my gosh."

"You're Snow White."

I stick my tongue out at her. "I'm Merida. I don't look anything like Snow White. And besides, isn't it Sleeping Beauty who has the birds? She sings with them."

"I defer to the elementary school teacher." She coaxes one of the green birds down her arm to the cup. "I'm sure you're the expert in cartoons."

"You'd be surprised how quickly the Disney stuff is fading." Or maybe I'm just surprised at what it's like to have a conversation without having to watch for barbs and sensitive spots. "I don't know, maybe I shouldn't say things like that. The kids I teach aren't exactly run of the mill."

"Tell me?" It's gentle coaxing, not an order.

I breathe deeply, wondering where to start. The bird on my hand dips to drink, and I make the same squeaking noise, then follow it up with a giggle. I'm a wind-up sound box, but I can't get my brain to make any reasonable response. "The kids I work with are totally normal in some ways—dead-on with the developmental scales and the full spectrum between whip smart and regular-old kids. It's the world of privilege they're in that's absolutely mind-blowing."

"Give me an example."

"I only spent a week couch surfing with a friend." This feels like some sort of confession. Like maybe I should have done more penance for leaving someone at the altar. Well, leaving them in a hotel room before we got to the altar, at least. "After that, I got an offer from the Lowensteins. Their son Barrak was in my class last year. They said they have a room I can use as long as I like."

Cai slides me a look out the corners of her eyes. She runs a single fingertip down the downy head of the bird on her forearm. "I feel like their definition of 'a room' and my definition are going to be completely different."

"It's an apartment over the detached garage. Have you ever seen *Sabrina*?"

"The old one or the new one?"

"With Audrey Hepburn."

"Yeah. I wanted to snatch Audrey away and tell her she could do so much better than a Humphrey Bogart who obviously didn't want to be there."

"I know, right? Total miscasting." I shake my head before I forget that I have a bird practically nesting in my curls. I have to push them back, away from his beak. He chirps in my ear. She? I have no idea what I'm dealing with here. "I've got four rooms with a full kitchen and a view of the pool."

"And they can just give it to you?"

"More or less. I've set a personal goal of getting out in three months, but Mrs. Lowenstein said I could finish out the school year. And that only started two weeks ago!"

"Come here," Cai says. She nudges the bird on her arm toward my left shoulder, the free one.

"I have a cape of birds." I laugh.

"It's great. Hold still." She pulls out her cell phone and snaps a couple of shots.

I try not to duck and run. It's hard to look directly at the lens. I don't always manage, looking away to the trees where dozens more birds are waiting. My smile is impossible to contain though, and honestly I don't really try. It feels too good to let loose.

I don't have a lot of experience with letting loose. The tattoo around my calf was probably the first time in five years that I managed it. Before that had been coming to California for school, but then I'd backed away from the reality of hard choices and adaption by hiding in the tempest Jody created for me.

I lift my hand and slowly turn my palm to the sky. The bird on my wrist travels with me until it's standing in my palm. There's a shaft of sunshine over both of us. I really am Sleeping Beauty or something. If only I could sing. "This is so fun."

"I'm glad." Cai's hair slides like silk from her shoulder to cascade down her chest. Her neat, pleat-front shirt catches black strands. "It'd really suck if I brought you here and then it turned out you were afraid of birds."

"Who's afraid of birbs?" I coo at the green friend standing on my hand. "Birbs are adorabubbles. Tumblr says so."

"Meme addict."

"Only the good ones."

I like the way she looks at me. I can't put my finger on what it is, but it makes me feel . . . appreciated. Wow. That's such a sad state of affairs. I crave being appreciated. That's not something that I should have been missing considering I was hours away from being married.

Next time. I'm not screwing it up next time. I'll pick someone who looks at me the way Cai looks at me. It can't be her, since she's made it perfectly clear she likes things uncomplicated, and I know I'm not ready for diving back in to forever. I don't deserve forever with someone if I can't keep Jody out of my thoughts for more than ten minutes. It's like she haunts me. My own personal Jack the Ripper. I'm mentally looking over my shoulder every three seconds, wondering what it is about me that made her select me. Made her choose me as the kind of girl who could be bowled over and used.

A polite announcement that the facility will be closing in fifteen minutes floats from concealed speakers among the trees. I put the cup of nectar on my palm so my particular bird friend can finish it off. I love his weird, tube tongue.

"You're a silly bird," I coo. "Aren't you? You like it in here? Do you like your tribe? Got a girlfriend?"

"Nope, I don't," Cai answers.

I laugh. "Gosh, I should hope not, or it would be really cruddy of you to invite me out."

"No worries." She pulls closer to me, wrapping an arm around my waist. The birds on my shoulder flutter away, but then one comes back to land on Cai's head. "Crap! What the hell!"

Her words are filled with laughter, not sharpness.

"Here, hold still." I try to shoo it away, but it's got its finger-claw things wrapped in Cai's black hair. "Get off her."

"I don't think it speaks English."

"Maybe the problem is that I don't speak lorikeet."

"You should get on that." She gives it a little push, but it doesn't like that. It lets out a string of chirping. "I think I just got cussed out in lorikeet."

My blood pressure is rising enough that my ears are tingling. I gulp. "Come on, birdie. It's locked tight. I'm sorry."

"It's not your fault," Cai says, and then she hands me her empty cup of nectar. "Here, hold that. Maybe he'll get away from me if I don't have anything good."

Except the worst happens.

I see his tail feathers lift and flutter, and I don't know how, but I know what he's going to do before it happens. Every cell I have cringes. The world slides sideways into slow motion. I flap my hands at the bird, and Cai's face contorts into confusion, but it's too late. Oh, too late.

The bird poops. The bird poops all down the back of Cai's perfect hair. It oozes. I die. Utter mortification makes me into a human goo pile. I can't freaking believe this.

"Oh! Oh, I'm so sorry!"

"Not your fault, baby." The bird finally launches away and flies to a close-by branch. I feel like it's taunting us with loud tweets. I frown at it. "How bad is it?" she asks me.

"Oh. Um." I lift my hands as if I'm going to wipe it away, but then pull back at the last second. There's no way I'm touching the viscous, sticky stuff. There's flecks in it. Poop covers the back of her head. "Yeah, not great."

"Putting a helmet on is going to be so not cool."

"I'm so sorry!" I catch my hands together, linking my fingers. "So sorry!"

"You have zero responsibility in this situation. I promise."

I don't understand. Her mouth is turned into a smile and her dark eyes are twinkling. It's like she really means it. "I should have pushed it off you faster."

"I have two perfectly able-bodied hands. I could have done it too. But, come on, I need a bathroom ASAP."

We find her one just outside the lorikeet enclosure. She bends over the sink to rinse her head, and I help as best I can. The dribble of the low-usage faucet is about as warm as a coffee that's been sitting out for an hour.

"At least it's not frigid," Cai says.

"That's being generous."

"As long as I don't get bird poop in my eyes, I can afford to be generous."

That makes me laugh, but I feel like I shouldn't, so I bite my lip and hold it in. Cai peeks up at me from between damp chunks of hair. "You can laugh. I look like a goofball."

"Maybe."

"Definitely."

"Well. If you insist." I release my giggles. The way I can only see one of her eyes peeking out from between hanks is incredibly absurd. "You look pretty damn ridiculous."

"There we go. Now scrub while you make fun of me."

I get a handful of paper towels and go back to wiping away what Cai can't see. We're both laughing, which makes it a hundred percent okay with me. I get closer and closer to her, until we're hip to hip. It's just for convenience at first, so I don't lose my balance leaning over her and the counter . . . and then it's more.

There's heat between us. Our feet become intertwined somehow, layered over so that the toes of her boots are against the arch of my sneaker. It's the barest bit of pressure, but it's in a place where I don't know I've ever connected with another human being. A variety of footsie that I know I haven't experienced before. Or if I did, it didn't feel like this. Sure as heck wasn't overwhelming enough to obliterate the fact that I'm washing *bird poop* out of my date's hair.

"I am so, so sorry," I say again. She peeks up at me and doesn't say anything, but I can hear her telling me to stuff it. I blush a little. "I can't help it. I was bred to be polite. Especially to my elders. Nanna Ethel saw to it."

"Elders? I am so going to make you regret that."

"I don't believe you." I get a wad of paper towel from the dispenser on the wall and wrap it around Cai's hair so she can stand up.

She takes the brown paper from me and scrubs her head. "Did I get it all?"

"Bend down?" I like how much taller than me she is. It's only five or six inches, but it's enough for me to enjoy my girliness. I gently squeeze out the wet. She lets me, rather than taking over the job. I like feeling useful to her. "Yeah, I don't see anything. I'd still probably take a Silkwood shower if I were you. All the scrubbing, head to toe."

"Want to join me?"

"No way!" I shake my head. "That is not appealing. Nuh-uh."

"Okay, fine." She catches me by the waist, pulling me closer. "Want to join me once I'm clean and shiny?"

My blood thickens and settles in my pussy. I lick my lips, and my mouth feels as dry as if I've been eating sand. Swallowing is hard. It's not that we're pelvis to pelvis, or at least not only that. It's the strong way she has hold of me and also the way she's looking at me. She's hungry. For me. It's hard to believe that someone as beautiful as her would even want me. But I can't deny what I see. Her lips are parted and I want to taste her.

I don't know where I find the courage, but I lean forward and press an open kiss to her plump bottom lip. I trace my tongue over her satin skin. "My place is close. Only a few miles away. It's about forty minutes."

"I bet I can make it less than that on my bike."

"I'd like that."

chapter

TANSY

The ride to my apartment is exhilarating. I've never felt speed in the same way as this. I'm learning to trust Cai's command of the motorcycle. She holds it between her legs as if it's an extension of herself and her soul. The buzz works into my bones and then becomes a part of me. The scents and sounds of the city flood in on me but then are gone again before I can even grasp them.

Cai dips between cars enough that I feel we're being risky, but not so much that it really feels dangerous. When she passes a Volvo, I get a glimpse of the middle-aged driver scowling at us. I laugh and blow a kiss. His eyes go wide, but then he's in our dust. It's blissful.

I can be big and bold too. I can be someone strong. It's inside me, and it's just been waiting to break free. I'm dying a small death and restarting my entire existence all over again. I wish I could ride with my arms thrown wide and only my faith in Cai's driving holding me steady, but I'm not ready for that.

Instead I turn my face upwards. It's the same whooshing excitement as being on a rollercoaster for the first time. The feeling that I don't really know what's coming, and I'm perfectly content with that.

It's not a thing I've felt very often.

Even back home in Idaho, I tried to map every step. It was safer that way when I had such a big secret to hide. Just because my family was okay with me being gay didn't mean that the rest of my small town would be comfortable with it. It was easier to live a careful life. I was lucky to even have Beth in town to be my first girlfriend. Otherwise it's been only Jody.

And now I'm going to have Cai.

She slows down as she pulls into my neighborhood and cruises through the wide boulevards. "How is it all this green? Hasn't anyone told them about water conservation?"

She has a serious point. The lawns are emerald green and palms aren't the only trees. It takes a lot of water to sustain this level of lushness. At the same time, I sometimes forget that this is unusual. It's this green back home, after all. "I think their water bills must be more expensive than my car payment."

"At least."

GPS tells her where to pull to the curb, and then I point over her shoulder at the carriage house. "Over there. Park on the west side."

There's a spot designated for me, but of course I left my car parked down the street from the restaurant. I'll have to go get it tomorrow. Will that count as a walk of shame? I'm a little bit excited. I've never done one before.

My legs are wobbly when I climb off Cai's motorcycle, and it's only partially because of the strength I used to hold on to her hips. Cai secures her helmet first, then the one I hand her, and then she reaches out for me.

I go into her arms as easily as breathing. We're sheltered between the ivy-covered brick of the carriage house and the equally ivy-covered fence at the edge of the Lowenstein's property line. I read *The Secret Garden* as a child. Places like this, tucked away from the world, can create their own sort of magic.

Cai holds my face between her hands. Her fingers are shaking, which makes my breasts tighten in response. We're so keyed up. My eyes dance, trying to take in each line and inch and color of her features. Her mouth is a firmer line than I would have expected.

If she's gearing up to say something serious, I don't want to hear it. I place my fingertips on her mouth. "Don't have second thoughts before we even have firsts."

"Tansy . . ."

"Let's go shower."

I lace her fingers through mine and tug her toward the wrought-iron and rosewood door that leads to my private stairs. My apartment is the top floor of the garage. Most of my belongings are still haphazardly stacked in boxes, even though I've been here close to two months. It's hard to bring myself to unpack when I know everything inside the boxes is such a jumble. I shoved everything in as fast as I humanly could while Jody was away from the apartment. I hired a service that specialized in emergency move-outs. They had my whole life packed up in less than a day.

If I'd been home in Idaho, it wouldn't have been like that. I'd have had people ready to help me.

When I open each box, I don't know what memories to prepare myself for. Sometimes I can't do it.

I ignore it all, and blissfully Cai doesn't ask any questions. I don't even flick on the lights as we go. The sun coming through the uncurtained windows is plenty, even in my bedroom.

I stop just inside the door. "I should get you a towel."

"You should get a few towels."

She's so sure of herself. I gulp and nod. My excitement and my nerves are warring for control of me, but it's my pussy that throbs with need and sneaks in to win the day. "This way," I say, and Cai follows me again.

I think this may be the only time the rest of the afternoon that Cai will be following me instead of the other way around.

The bathroom was redone a few years ago and shows it. The sink is a bowl above the line of the counter that looks lovely now but will scream mid-2010s in a few years. It won't matter, since the Lowensteins will quickly have it remodeled.

I love the shower. It's such a huge expanse of tile and space that there's no need for anything so tacky as a curtain or a sliding glass door. That would be entirely beneath Essie Lowenstein's taste. Most of the bathroom is tiled in pale-gray herringbone, but the shower is slightly sunken and delineated with ocean pebbles sliced flat to make mosaic tile. Fluffy towels are rolled and waiting in a square teak basket at the edge.

I make myself busy flicking the water on. The main showerhead is square, but there's also a handheld option. "It's nice, right? Essie's mother lived here for a few years, but then she decided Southern California wasn't warm enough for her. She moved to Boca Raton. I'm lucky they don't believe in renting out."

"'Don't believe' . . ." Cai echoes me, but then trails off. "What does that even mean?"

"They don't trust randos on their property?" I shrug. "They're rich as Croesus. Albert Lowenstein made his money in plastics and then came out to California in the sixties to work hand in hand with Boeing. It's his son who runs everything now. Timothy."

"I don't think my mom ever knew that much about my teachers or my teachers knew that much about us. I guess we'd have been a way more boring story."

Her words choke off, and I freeze with my fingertips in the rain spray of the faucet. I can hear her unspoken words. A boring story . . . *until*. I can't imagine how effectively such an event must have marked her family as definitively as AD or BC. Except instead of *anno Domini*, theirs really would have been *after death*.

I don't know if I'd have been able to ever get out of bed if I'd been Cai. Certainly not if I'd been Cai's mother. The sheer injustice of my daughter's destruction at the hands of a madman would be enough to make me scrabble for bottles of pills. Go to bed and never get up.

The tantalizing flavor of too many Xanax rides on the edge of my tongue. It'd be so sour that I'd have to resist the urge to vomit. A dangerous pleasure. Something that can't be found and will never be lost. It lurks in the dark and waits for me to get too sleepy to defend myself.

I push it all away. I'm not there. It's far enough gone that I'm okay now. I'm fine.

When I turn around and physically look away from my past, Cai is my reward.

She's naked, in a way. The tattoos decorating her skin are her only protection. Her slacks are a pool of gray pinstripe on the tile, and she's standing in front of them. A pair of vaguely boy-style briefs covers her hips and her mons. Her button-down shirt seems as gone as a will-o'-the-wisp, or at least I can't seem to look away long enough to spot it. Because, oh, her breasts are glorious. Absolutely perfect.

I'm drawn closer to her. I'm half afraid to touch the swaths of ink across her hips and waist and arms, but once I manage to begin, it's like she's been inked with magnets. I can't stay away. My hands lift and cup her tits. Her nipples fit exactly in the crease between my thumb and palm. My fingers cover her skin. She's pale brown with warm undertones, but a lighter version than along her arms and face and neck. Cai is not a friend of the sunshine, but she doesn't seem the least bit ashamed of that even though we live in a sun-mad world.

She pushes the thick sheaf of her still-damp black hair so that it falls down her back. She's giving me every inch of her skin that I'd like to take. When she lets her hips shift, she lifts her breasts into my touch.

I skim over her. This is a miracle and she's a fairy. Wait, I think that's mixing up religion and myth. Am I breathing? I feel as lightheaded as if I've been holding my breath, but I think, if anything, I'm practically panting. My heartbeat is such a rush it feels like one swelling pulse that owns me.

Maybe Cai owns me.

I bite my lip since I can't think of anything appropriate to say. She makes a noise in the back of her mouth and cups my jaw. Her thumb brushes over my lip, pulling it away from my teeth. "Little one."

It doesn't sound like a question, but it feels like one. "Yes."

"I'm going to shower. Come to the edge. Wait for me."

"Okay." I find myself nodding as she walks past me.

She pushes down her panties as she walks. They cling to her hips for a moment, and then she keeps walking, and they fall to the floor without even trying to trip her up. It's like watching a magic trick made of seduction.

Even her bum is a perfect upside-down heart. The curves draw my eye toward the center of her back, where two little dimples wait. I want to drop to my knees to worship them with my tongue.

I'm practically dizzy with so much want. I hardly know what to do with myself. This isn't like me. I always had to be coaxed before, nudged out of my shell and told what to do next. I had vague want and they filled in the pieces.

This time I know I need to taste Cai. I need to lick her clit and feel her wetness slide over my chin more than I need to breathe.

I put my hand out to the wall. It's cool to the touch, which manages to center me a little bit.

Cai steps under the water fall like a queen, with her shoulders held back and her spine so straight that I can read the words inked there. *In Memoriam, 1976–1996.* That must be her sister. Only twenty. That would have been so horrific on every level.

The water pours over Cai's hair, locking the strands into a thick hank. It hits her angle-sharp shoulders next and casts off into open space before the next rush of water curves lovingly over the tops of her arms. She turns her face up to the spray and lifts her hands to her hair.

She's a Degas statue with one knee lifted and the near backwards curve of her other leg. The shadow of hair over her vagina makes her into even more of a mystery. My fingers scrabble for purchase on the wall, but there's nothing but the barest gap. I touch rock instead of her flesh.

It's killing me. I can't look away from her, but she told me to wait, and I don't think I was supposed to look away anyway. I don't want to. I want her.

I open my mouth to speak, then bite down on the tip of my tongue because I can't think of any words that are as perfect as she looks.

I wish I was an artist. A painter, a sculptor. Anything that could even try to capture her beauty.

A drop of glimmering water breaks free of the sheet across her shoulder and slides down its own path. I wonder how that works, what brief break of skin and hair and magic can release a single drop from the mass of the rest. I could chase that path with my tongue. I will if given a chance.

She takes her time looking through my small selection of toiletries. When she opens the cap of my conditioner and smells it, she looks back at me. "So this is why you smell like cotton candy."

My cheeks steal heat from the throb between my thighs. "My body wash is really sweet too. Is that bad?"

"No." It's only one word, but I know just from the way she says it that it's more than that. She loves the way I smell. "It makes me want to eat you up."

My fingers are shaking. Some women would have a sophisticated response to that. I squeak, "Okay."

She grins, then turns back to the spray. It's strange to watch a new woman wash. She goes in a different order than I do, soaping up her body before washing her hair. In the steamy heat of the room, I can't remember what Jody did, and I can't bring myself to care in the least. This is about Cai. This is what I'm making with Cai.

It's not long before she's clean and smelling as sweet as I normally do. I grab a towel from the basket and hold it open. She steps into the curve of my attention, and I'm confused for a moment when she doesn't take it for herself. She only watches me with a small smile curving her soft mouth.

I dry her off with tender pats over every inch of her. Her shoulders and back are easy. I circle her to get everything. She's lean all over, and a small striation dives from the side of her waist toward the front of her stomach. I'm breathing in choppy bursts through my parted lips. I wonder if she can feel my air and the way she owns it all.

I fold to my knees to dry her toned calves. Even with the shaggy gray bathmat, the floor is hard and I still don't care. When I take the towel up between her thighs, I can't keep my shaking hidden. I think she likes it. Her eyes smolder.

Her hand comes to rest on my head. It's the lightest weight of fingertips and a strand or two of my flyaway hair caught on her nails. My heart tumbles and lifts at the same time. I try to squeeze my thighs together against the delicious ache between them, but it's not nearly enough.

"Would you lick my pussy here?" Her hand moves over the crown of my head. I'm torn between letting my eyes flutter shut and making sure they stay peeled open so I don't miss a moment of this. "It's got to hurt your knees, doesn't it?"

"I would." I don't want to talk about the hurt, about the small part of me that might like it that way. This is so strange and different and amazing all at once. The pain would cement the difference, make sure I didn't mistake this time with Cai for anything else I've had before.

What the last time was like.

I wasn't there last time. The way my knees are grinding keeps me present. I like it that way. I don't want to get lost somewhere else.

She watches me as hard as I watch her. It's like she's trying to crawl inside my brain. I only want to show her certain parts. The rest of it would change this moment. So I lean forward and press my lips to the small knob of her pelvic bone.

Her skin is thinner than satin and smoother than silk. I taste clean, soft water. It's hard, but I don't immediately dive in to tasting her center. She hasn't given me permission. Instead I kiss a line of worship from her hip to her knee, sinking farther back into my position until my bum is on my heels and my head is fully bent before her. I hold her calf and rest my forehead against her knee. She's sharp and soft at the same time.

"Tell me what to do." I finally close my eyes. If I'm holding on to her, I know where I am. "Tell me. Please."

Twelve

Tansy

For a long, heartbreaking moment, I worry that she's going to pull back from me. I've pushed things too far and asked for too much. My life is a chain of moments where I'm always too much or not enough.

But then her touch slides from my head to the top of my neck. She twines her fingers through my hair, not quite gathering a ponytail of it, but instead making it hers. Owning me by way of her grip on my curls. I shiver. She twists tighter. The kiss of pinch across my scalp centers me right where I am. "Do you often play this way?"

I shake my head even though it makes my scalp hurt. Maybe because of it, exploring the resistance. "Never."

"Then I need to lay this out: do you want me to be in charge?"

I want her to be in charge of all of me, but I know I can't ask for that. And maybe when I come out of this haze right here, the mysterious waves of desire throbbing through me, I'll get over that too. But for right now this feels momentous. "I do."

The vows I didn't say two months ago. I make a noise and bury my face against her thigh. She's too skinny to hide me, so instead I pull some of her strength into myself.

"Do you want to serve me?"

"I do." The tips of my breasts are so hard they're tingling. I don't think I could want anything else more. Every bit of me is right here, curled up against her leg like a toy. Like a pet. I'm her servant. Even the fact that she's naked and I'm clothed doesn't matter. The skirt I'd had to tie up to ride her motorcycle now pools around our feet, and it's just another way we're linked together.

Her hand clenches in my hair. It's a promise and a response all at once. I need it; I need to know how much she needs me. "You're a good girl. Such a sweet angel."

The words unlock a part of me that's been lonely for so long. The back of my eyes sting and prickle with tears. I don't want to cry. This isn't a crying time.

I press my lips against the side of her knee instead. The skin there is more like the delicate web over her hip bone rather than what's at the front of her knee. I dart a lick in order to taste the difference. She's the pale nothing taste of water. I need something more than that. I nuzzle my way upward.

She's standing with her feet only a little bit apart. I kiss my way up her thighs. She's not stopping me. Every half inch makes my mouth water a little more. The tops of her thighs are dusted with fine dark hair as soft as baby's breath. It tickles over my parted lips.

I'm only one more kiss away from her pussy when her grip on my hair twists tight. I whimper. Holy crud, I actually make an involuntary whimper. I crave her that badly. If she's wet, if I lick between her lips, then I'll know that she's here as much as I am.

She jerks my head so that I'm looking up at her. The shift in perspective is dizzying. "Your word is banana," she says.

I only blink, then lick my bottom lip. I'm distracted by the artful droop of her breasts from this angle. They're small, but from here I see nothing but their curve and the dark brown of her nipples. They're so hard that her areola have all but disappeared, clenched into nubs that I want to suck on. "What?"

"If you need anything to stop, or even slow down a little bit." She's breathing hard enough that I watch her chest rise and fall. "Your safeword is banana."

I can't imagine how I'd need a safeword just for finally being able to do what I've desired for so long. But she called me a good girl and I don't want to ruin that. "Okay."

Should I add some title to the end of that? *Ma'am* doesn't feel right, but using her name feels almost weirdly intimate. Like we'd be on an even ground that I don't want right now. I settle for stupidly repeating myself.

She doesn't seem to mind. Her feet shift wider, moving her legs apart, keeping her grip on my hair. I test her, trying to look away from her gaze, but she doesn't let me go. I think I like it this way. I want to see her, to taste her and feel her under my tongue, but I want it on her terms. Everything is safer that way.

Her scent rises to me. My mouth waters. I feel a surge of heat in my own pussy, and I'm startled to be reminded of my active desire for sex. This isn't all about what I want to do to her. How strange and beautiful.

"Describe what you're going to do."

"I'm going to give you oral sex."

She giggles, a husky laugh. I blush, and I'd look away from her, but I can't. Not with the way she's holding me. Suddenly I feel the pain spiking up from my knees.

"You're so fucking cute," she says, and the pain goes away.

I want to hear more, but I don't know how to ask. I cycle through five different ways to phrase it before settling on the simplest. Maybe it won't sound egotistical. Maybe it will and I'll see a disappointed flash in her eyes. I risk it. "Why?"

"Because even now you don't say it the dirty way. You're going to eat me out."

"I am," I agree. But I don't think I can say it on my own.

"I like it." She traces a single fingertip over the curve of my cheek. "You're so pure. An innocent."

It's the first thing said that makes me want to pull away. But with the way she's holding me, I can only drop my gaze to her navel. "I'm not."

"You are."

"There's things . . ." Things that happen in the night, with only my cat watching and the dark not protecting me. The smell of a couch that I'd eaten pizza and watched movies on. The life that I used to have coming apart at the seams. "'Innocent' is for kids."

"No, not always." She tickles a circle across my temple that makes me shiver. "Sometimes it's about what's in here."

"I don't want to talk about it."

"Fine." And, instantly, I can feel the backing off in the air. She means it. She's not hiding bullets behind her back.

I could get drunk on this woman. "May I?"

I wonder if she's going to make me say it. If she'll take perverse pleasure in having me ask in a naughty way. I could do it, if that's what she wanted, but I turn dirty words over in my mind and I don't think I'd have any excitement from them. They're only words that I've trained myself not to use. I don't think it matters that much, not really.

But she doesn't. "You may."

Two simple words. I suck in a breath of joy that's thick with her musky scent. I lean forward the few, bare inches needed, and my knees rotate on the mat, and I don't care at all at the jolt that runs through me. I have my purpose.

I press a close-mouthed kiss to the curls that protect her still-closed body. My mouth comes away wet with her slickness. I lick my lips and want more. She tastes fantastic. A little salty, just slightly tart.

The hand I have at her knee slides up and up, and then I have a grip on the swell of her ass. There I find more of her hidden softness. I feel like I'm grasping for a life raft rather than holding her still. I'm not the one in charge here.

I lick her with the flat of my tongue. Her hair abrades me, then she opens, and I'm deep in her taste and, goodness, it's good. Oh, it's so good. My eyes close. My nose is against her body. My mouth is open on her. I'm doing my best to bury myself in her. To lose myself in this act.

It's so right, and it only gets better when she moans. It's the time I shove my tongue against her clit that makes another sound come from her, so I do it again. Then again.

She parts her legs further, which gives me more room and also brings her down an inch or two closer to me. I take and take. She is so wet, it rolls down my chin. I lick her inside and out and over again. It's an eternity in the best kind of way, where time spools and unwinds.

At some point I lose track of what it is that gets the best sounds from her. I spend my time in exploration for the pure greed of it. I want to know the inside of her thighs, where the muscles twitch and tendons shift. I need to feel her from the inside out when I push my tongue deep in her. It's my own cravings that make me suck her clit between my lips and flick it.

Cai holds my head between both her hands. I know if I try to pull away she wouldn't let me, but she's not hurting me either. "You're hella fucking good at that, you know."

I didn't know that. Am I actually good or are these the sweet words that come on the crest of an orgasm? I know Cai is looking at me, not through me. She knows who it is kneeling before her. She's here with me.

My hands clench tight on her butt. *Please don't leave me*, I want to say, so I write the words against her flesh instead. *I would give you everything.* I didn't think I could be this person again so quickly. My neediness must be a weight. I give her more sensation instead. My chin rubs against her gate while I carve patterns against her swollen, hot clit.

I lift up on my knees on purpose. They hurt. They sting. I drive the pain into my bones at the same time I lick Cai from the bottom to the tops of her lips.

Cai pushes her hands into my hair and scoops it up. Air flows across my bare neck, and it's surprisingly cold. I jolt toward her. Cai scrapes her nails across my bare shoulders. She goes lightly at first, and it doesn't hurt. The repetition over the same path begins to sting. She doesn't move her track. I don't stop what I'm doing.

She might mark me. I don't care.

She catches the top of my blouse, dragging it across my skin and getting tangled in a way that she can't scratch me to her satisfaction. She flicks the strap. "Take this off."

I whimper and push my face into her body until my lashes brush against her pubic hair. I keep licking. I don't want to stop.

She catches my hair and twists. "I said take it off. Your shirt first. Grab the hem and pull it over your head. Next you'll push down your skirt."

I look up, up her body, and she's watching me with narrowed eyes that are so fucking hot. She liked my defiance, I think, but she likes even more that she can still tell me what do to.

I am so fucking relieved to not have to guess, even down to the how. It strips away my fear of screwing up. I obey.

Obey.

The echo pings around my head, but at the same time I'm newly naked before her.

I completely ease into my folded position so that my butt is back on my heels. It gives momentary respite to my knees. I don't know what it says about me that I'm not sure I want that.

This is a pose I've never tried before. She doesn't know it, but this is a thing that I can give Cai that's precious and untouched.

I fold my hands in my lap. My thighs are pressed together. My panties are such a pale blue that they might look white and my bra matches. When I dressed for this date, I wasn't intentionally thinking about sex, but I dressed to please Cai. I'd said such a stupid thing, and I hated myself for screwing up something fantastic.

Except I think I've made up for it. I hide my naughty smile. Cai is taking me in. I don't want to change the vibe of this moment. Not with the way her eyes are so hungry.

Hungry for me. It's mind-blowing.

She rubs the backs of her fingers over my cheek. "You definitely look like an angel."

"I didn't think you were religious."

"I didn't think I was either."

Her fingers coast over my cheek to my temple and across my forehead. I don't know that anyone else has ever touched me between my brows before, and when she slides down the slope of my nose, it tickles. I let my eyes shut, and even my lids become hers to touch. She's blind and I'm mute and together we're practically one person.

She eases forward until she's standing above me. "Make me come, little one."

I've been little and small before, but it didn't feel like this. It was always dangerous to be small before. Not now. I'm protected in the shelter of Cai's body. She has my hair gathered up again, and she's holding me as delicately as I could ever hope. But her other hand is clutching my shoulder like she doesn't want to let me go.

I open my mouth and steal her for myself. It's perverted communion, and I'm taking her body into my own.

"Use your hands," she orders in a husky voice.

I spread her lips and hold her flesh taut under my tongue. I lick, she shudders. More. Again. I circle her opening with two fingers, rubbing and rubbing and then sliding only an inch inside. She's textured and soaking wet, and I get all of this to revel in as what I've done to her.

I hold back my own surging wave of sensation. I'm so wet and swollen that tightening my pelvic muscles takes me shockingly close to coming. It all feels so good. Maybe I'm delusional, but each rub of my tongue over her clit makes my own clit surge in response. We're that interwoven.

I feel her orgasm start in the way her legs shake. Her grip on my shoulder holds tighter. I drop into a smooth rhythm between the licking and the way I'm taking her with my fingers. Point and counterpoint. Her quiet moans get louder.

"Fuck," she mutters. "Motherfucker, gonna be hard. Don't stop. Don't stop."

The order turns into a chant. I wouldn't dream of stopping, not now. Not when I have her here, balanced above me and it's trust for both of us. I lick and lick. Thrust my tongue against her body as if it's part of my soul. I can't give her more than this, so I'll give her everything this is.

She closes her hands across the back of my skull. My hair is woven through her fingers, which pull and tug. The pinch hurts and soothes. I shore up one of her legs by wedging my shoulder against her. She shudders in a body-wracking way.

"There. Fuck. Fuck!"

She's coming. Her girl juices paint my chin and my cheeks. A drop rolls down my neck, and I mourn its loss. I drink her deep as quickly as I can. This is sweeter than what she'd given me before. I lap away every last bit.

I'm cleaning her with my mouth when I realize she's petting my temples and cheeks and cooing sweet words at me. "My little one. I can't even. That was so much. So beautiful."

I had no shame when I was buried mouth-deep in her body, but for some reason hearing such niceness makes me die in the best kind of way. "Shush."

"It's so true." Her hands float over me like happy birds. "You're an angel to me. You're too good to me."

I shake my head because I have no words.

"I didn't even give you a towel to kneel on."

"I liked it," I whisper.

"What's that?"

I clear my throat, but I can't make myself look up at her, so I settle for her navel. It's shallow. I ring it with a fingertip, then realize the finger's still damp from Cai. I pop it in my mouth, not wanting to lose even a speck of her taste. "I liked not having padding."

A smile takes over her pleasure-soft mouth. "Who'd have thought such a wicked girl was hiding inside the angelic elementary school teacher."

Me. I knew. I've wanted something different and bigger. Maybe this is it. This thing I have with Cai is what I was looking for when I wandered into her shop to get a tattoo. "You're the one who inked me."

"I am. Maybe you need more. But later. Right now, feel what you've done to me."

She takes my hand and guides it to her pussy, and she's wet and I jerk back so hard that my knees go up. I accidentally catch the back of her knee and have to grab for the floor behind me to avoid falling. Cai's hand flies out and smacks flat against the wall. The echo is loud in the room that suddenly feels startlingly small.

"Sorry!" I yelp. "Sorry, sorry."

"What?" She's confused. Of course she is. I'm an idiot. "Are you okay?"

"I'm fine. I'm sorry."

"No, no, you're fine." She reaches for me again, and I flinch.

As if it'll make this situation any more sane, I push to my feet and dust off my butt. I'm still nearly naked. I still have traces of Cai's taste on my lips. I paste a giant smile on. Nothing about this is fooling Cai. "What do you want to do now?"

She narrows her eyes. Her hair is still damp. It hangs heavily about her face. She shoves a lock back behind her ear. "If there's something wrong, you can tell me."

I can't. Not because of anything about her, but because the words have claws that lodge in my throat and stay there. I don't even think them, which leaves me no way to speak them. "I'm fine. It's fine."

"If I crossed a line . . ."

It pushes through my haze. "No, you didn't." I move close enough that I'm back in Cai's sphere. My hands find the softness of her waist, the gentle padding below her belly button. "You were perfect. That was perfect."

She's watching me, but at the same time I can feel her willingness to believe me in the way her shoulders loosen and her spine softens. Her hips drift toward me. "That most certainly was perfect."

The last thing in the world I want is to ruin what just happened. If I have even the least little bit of control over myself, I'm not delving into the past. "Thank you," I say instead.

"No, Jesus Christ, thank *you*." She laughs, and at last I can smile. Her happiness is infectious.

I lay my head on her shoulder and wrap my arms around her waist. This is safety. I don't know how I got here, not really. Some miraculous set of coincidences, but however it happened, I don't want to leave.

Maybe not ever.

Thirteen

Cai

There's something going on here that I don't understand. I rub Tansy's back and wonder if she realizes she's trembling like she's the one who just had a world-changing orgasm. I don't think it's from a good source though. Not with the way she's hiding against me. She's caught in a web.

I didn't like Jody when I met her, and if possible, I like her even less now. This fragility is her fault. I'm sure of it.

I just don't know what to do about it.

"Let's go to your bedroom."

She nods, takes my hand, and leads me back the way we came in. This feels like an abnormal quiet, the kind of silence that isn't usual to cheery, happy Tansy. Unless this is the real her and what I've known before was an act? It's hard to parse the difference between truth and the pretty face people put on in the first flush of a new relationship. Sometimes I don't want to figure it out—but Tansy is different.

All of Tansy is different. It's not that she's fragile, it's that she keeps trying anyway. Keeps moving up.

I get more of a look around her room this time. Enough boxes line the north wall that it looks like a kid's fort. The bed is enormous and probably came with the room. Seafoam-green bed hangings draped from the tall posts coordinate with the darker gray-green walls. Piled on the nightstand is a stack of novels with cracked spines. On top of the stack is a coffee cup with a glittery unicorn pooping a rainbow.

Tansy makes a run for the side of the bed that's piled with clothes. She grabs big armfuls and tosses them onto the wing chair in the corner. "Sorry it's a mess. I haven't really settled in, and I didn't really know I'd be having company. I mean, I didn't really expect this. Us."

She waves a hand around the space between us. I catch her fingers, twining mine through hers. Her palm is hot and her skin delicate, but something in the middle of her palm catches my attention. I turn her hand upward and skim a touch over the center. "What's this?"

"Bunch of paper cuts." Her fingers twitch as if she's trying to yank away, but then she stills. She takes a deep breath. "From this morning. I was stacking supplies for the kids' project."

"I didn't know teaching was a dangerous job."

She pouts a little bit. "You don't have to mock me."

My eyebrows fly up. I dip my knees, trying to look at her expression. She seems serious. "I wasn't. I didn't mean to."

"Oh." Her pout doesn't go away though.

I cup her cheek and lay my thumb over that softened bottom lip. "What's going on with you?"

"I don't know. I'm a mess." She covers her face, her shoulders curling in. "I'm sorry. Ugh."

"Stop it." I peel her hands away, use them both to pull her closer to me. "You're in your head, aren't you? Thinking about something else?" Or someone else.

"I don't want to." Her eyes are huge. It almost seems like she's two breaths from crying again, which is such a switch from where we were moments ago. My brain is still hazed in afterglow, but she needs me. "I don't want to think about anything but you."

I sit on the edge of the bed, my feet on the floor. "Come here."

She comes close enough that our knees nudge and her toes stack on mine. "Will you make me feel good?" Her words come out in a whisper.

"I hope so." Christ, I really fucking hope so. I'm going to feel like a pile of shit if I fail her, especially after how good she made me feel.

I haul her into my lap so that she's sitting sideways. She folds around me, her head resting on my shoulder and her knees along my ribs. I wrap an arm around her back and tuck my other hand under her thigh. I pet her back and legs, running my fingers up and down in soft and gentle circles. She sighs and eases into my hold.

"I like the way you feel in my lap, little one." I speak the words into the cloud of her hair.

"I like it too." But then she opens her mouth over my neck and I get a sharp nip.

I pinch her neck and pull her back. "Don't be bad."

She's smirking a little. "Make me?"

"Are you a baby girl? A brat?"

A wrinkle twists her pale brows. "I don't know. Maybe? Tell me what you mean?"

"Daddy doms and little girls are a certain kind of thing. A way some people play tops and bottoms." I gentle the hold I have on the back of her neck but don't let her go completely. "I'm starting to think you've got some of that."

She bites her bottom lip. Pink flushes her mouth. "But that would make you my daddy? You are most certainly not a boy. How does that still work?"

I shrug and go back to petting her leg. She leans into me again, a little bit of her tension leaving with every breath. "It works however the fuck we want to define it. Maybe it just means I like taking care of my little girl." She shudders hard enough that her hip grinds against my pussy. "Oh, someone liked that, didn't she?"

She nods frantically. "Wow, yeah. I did. Can we do that? Try that?"

"We already are," I say, and then I kiss her so deeply that her head bends and she arches over the arm I have around her back.

She's beautiful and wrapped tighter than a spring. I drag my teeth down her neck. The tendons there stand in stark relief under her pale skin. At her collarbone, I trade teeth for tongue and follow the curved arch.

"You're so pretty, little one," I mutter against her.

She holds my shoulder. Her noises are a series of squeaks and breathy sighs, especially when I push her bra down enough to make a shelf for her tits. I suck the tip of her breast into my mouth and start with only tongue and lips against the tight bead of her nipple.

The areola surrounding is nubbly when I circle. I drink deep of her flesh and my reward is more of those welcome sounds.

The whole time, I keep up my gentle touching of her thighs. I want her used to me and on edge at the same time. "You squirm as if it's your first time."

"I'll try to stop," she says on panting breaths.

"Don't you fucking dare," I growl. "I like it."

That earns me a sound perilously close to a mewl. I laugh, but I'm sure it sounds like I'm strangling at the same time, because I practically am. I can't resist anymore. I delve between her legs and stroke the front of her panties.

She parts her legs for me. Her knees separate, and her foot scrabbles for purchase in the pillowy duvet. She's panting, and I can see why when the thin cotton instantly soaks through with her wetness.

"Good girl," I tell her. "You've been so patient, and you made me feel so good."

"I'm so glad."

Her bottom lip is wet. I take it in a kiss. My mouth owns her just as deeply as can be. I lick her lip into my mouth and suckle. She is so fucking pliable and receptive. I kiss her deeper, then deeper still, pressing into her mouth.

Her fingers dig and release on my shoulder. She's like a kitten who's found something soft to hold on to. I don't feel very damn soft though. Not with how hot and ready her pussy is.

I skim over her flat stomach and push under her panties. I could take them off, but for some reason I don't want to. Maybe because it feels filthier to be delving inside them like this, as if she's giving up something that maybe she doesn't want to. Like I'm taking. Combined with her pushed-down bra and the way her straps dangle around her shoulders, she looks completely demolished.

I've done this to her. And I'm going to do more.

I pet her outer lips, then stroke inside. Wetness makes everything slip and slide, but I manage to catch hold of her inner lips and pinch them together. She gasps, her eyes going wide.

"More of that, please," she says. Her voice is raspy and raw. "I like that."

"Like this?" I experiment with how tight I pinch, how fast, the pulsing between. "Which do you like best?"

"All of it. Oh, all of it." She's lifting her hips into everything I do.

"Then maybe I should play with your pretty little clit instead."

"Okay," she squeaks.

I hide my laugh because I don't think she'd take it in the spirit intended right now. She's so cute I could die of it. Instead I stroke the tight bit of flesh at the top of her pussy and pour my determination into it. She's writhing practically, and I love it.

She chants my name as she gets closer and closer to the edge. I lick and bite her neck. A smattering of freckles dot the landscape of her upper chest. I try to catch each one with my teeth. She's quaking. I rub her just a little bit harder.

It's enough. She cracks open into a cry. Her head thrown back, every muscle she has pulls tight. The curve of her stomach becomes a stiff board. Her thighs clench hard around my hand as if she's afraid I'll pull away.

I wouldn't dream of it. I ride out her orgasm with pleasure, making my touches softer and gentler with every twitch of her hips. I'm telling her how perfect she is, the sweetness of her skin, the way she's made of clouds and fucking moonbeams. The words spill from my mouth and across her body, and I hope she catches each one. I hope she soaks them up, because I hardly know what I'm saying and if I can ever repeat them.

She comes down slowly, but not even as slowly as I'd like. I want her to ride this train as long as she possibly can. But it's only minutes before her head rests against my shoulder. She's warm, and the places where our skin meets are sticky with heat and sweat. I push her hair back from her face.

"How are you?"

"Good," she says in a drowsy tone.

"Here, let's tuck you in." I shuffle us around until she's lying flat on her bed.

She blinks slowly, and her lashes barely come up again. Her lids are sleepy and heavy. "But I'm not tired." She rubs her eyes with the side of her hand.

"I can see that." I hide my grin and line myself up beside her. I throw a leg over both of hers. "Just be still for a little while."

"Kay." Her breathing is shallow and rapid, but she seems to be quickly dropping off into sleep anyways. I unsnap her bra and ease it down from its awkward position so it won't hurt her. She works with me but doesn't open her eyes. Then she shifts onto her side, catching my hand as she goes and hooking my arm around her waist.

I'm pulled into spooning her. Not that I try very hard to get away. She's made of softness. I let her curls cover my face. She smells like cotton candy and something warm that's got to be exclusively her. I breathe deep. Let the moment spill into the quiet of contentment. Cars occasionally drive by outside, but they're far enough away that they only add to the hum of the city. In the next room, her cat meows. I wonder if it'll come out and visit.

Our breathing nearly echoes in the empty, unlived in space that surrounds us. This is the world that Tansy is floating in. A great gray between. I want to give her more than this, and I want to run away at the same time. This is a life I don't belong in. This is a room that's too big and grand, and this isn't how a one-bedroom crash pad is supposed to look. It's decorated with style and grace. The Lowenstein family took Tansy in and offered her an apartment that thousands of Angelenos would kill for. I wonder if she even realizes the level of privilege involved. When I was twenty-one, I left a girlfriend on two days' notice. I ended up sleeping on the floor of a friend's apartment, wrapped in a sleeping bag with a broken zipper for three and a half weeks.

Tansy ended up in an apartment with a bathroom decorated like a spa. We're worlds apart, and I should leave her here in this pretty world she gets.

But I keep holding her. I don't go away.

I don't know if I can. Not now, at least.

Not this moment. Not with the dreams I can taste on the tip of my tongue.

chapter

Fourteen

TANSY

I come up from sleep fighting. Hands flailing, stomach tight, I ratchet up into a seated position. I'm gasping. Air is thick, and I'm in the dark, and my hand lands on something soft like flesh. I fly out of the bed.

"Chill, chill," says a voice I recognize.

"Cai?"

"It's me. I'm right here. It's just dark."

I wrap my arms around myself. She'd been pressed against me, and I didn't know who it was. "Did I hurt you? I'm sorry."

"I'm fine. Are you?"

My eyes are starting to adjust to the dark. She's reaching for me. I want to reach back, but for a long second, I can't make myself move. I'm in a different dark. Gyoza twines around my ankles. She's sleek and soft, a reassurance that I'm exactly where I'm supposed to be.

I catch Cai's hand and let her pull me down to the bed.

The small of my back is cold with sweat. I swallow down my fear and try to pretend there's nothing wrong with me.

I wish there was nothing wrong with me.

"I'm fine." I'm stiff as a board. I lie flat, but my shoulders are pulling up toward my ears. I try to take a deep breath, but I'm also trying to keep Cai from noticing, and it's so awkward. Since I've been in this apartment, I've been falling asleep with my iPad playing TV shows I've already seen. If I wake up in the middle of the night, it's a comforting glow and familiar voices. It's really dark tonight.

There must not be any moon out. "I have to work tomorrow. It's a school day."

There's a long pause that I don't know how to fill. "Do you want me to go?"

"No, but I'm just warning you. I get up at like five."

"Really?"

No, not really. I'm lying through my liar teeth and I don't know why. I can't make my mouth shut. "Yeah, I like to be in my classroom around six thirty."

Holy crud, there go more lies. Lightning is going to strike me dead. God's going to tell me to get going once I get to the pearly gates.

"I sleep in." She rubs my arm, and I know part of me could respond. I could turn my face and kiss her mouth, and she'd start us all over again. Maybe that's what I need. What I want. "It's what comes with having such late hours usually."

"We're ships passing in the night?" I wish I would stop saying stupid stuff, but there's panic at the back of my throat and I can*not* stop. "I don't want to wake you up too early."

"Maybe I should go."

"No," I say, but *Yes*, I think.

And she hears the silent me. She pushes up until she's sitting, then bends down to kiss me. We taste like sleep twined together, but then she pulls back. "Shit, your car."

"I'll get a Lyft. I have a credit. I referred a friend," I say in a rush. Because when I lie, I always pile it on thick? I'm such an idiot.

"I can't let you do that."

I have zero interest in getting on a motorcycle at this hour, but I have no freaking clue how to say that to her. For a brief moment, I consider rolling onto my side and feigning sleep. Maybe it will work if I pull my pillow over my head. I don't know if I can sleep without a light, though.

Alternate plan. I shove myself into Cai's personal space instead. Head on her shoulder, arm across her ribs, my hips against her thigh. I make a noise like I'm so very tired even though every nerve in my body is on high alert. "I'm so tired."

"Uh-huh." She's not buying it, but she's not pushing me either. Instead she curls her arms around me. Her chin comes to rest on the top of my head. "Sleep, little one. Just sleep."

Except of course I can't. I've painted myself into a corner. I'm practically vibrating with awakeness. Is that even a word? I don't care. I can't figure a way out of this. "Tell me about your sister."

And poof, just like that. she's as stiff as I am frantic inside my head. "Xue?"

It's cruelly reckless, but either I'll understand her a little better or she'll pull away and leave me safe in my quiet darkness. "Yeah."

Silence spins out for one breath, then three. I'm not sure which way she's going to break, and then she drags in a breath that's slow and deep and too shaky for saying she's off, thanks for the good time. "She was so fucking brilliant. Everything my parents wanted. The perfect daughter."

"But you weren't?"

She doesn't answer. I picture her staring at the ceiling. I hate the dark. It's heavy. I feel it on my skin and in the way I try to fill in the shadows with what I should be able to see.

"She was in pre-med and acing it. She worked so hard. Her whole world revolved around studying. I was already partying a little bit. Having her as my older sister meant that I couldn't measure up no matter what, so I sort of stopped trying."

"Going to parties doesn't mean you're not trying." I play with the ends of her hair. I love how long it is. At some point she must have gotten out of bed, because she's wearing her boy-cut panties again. I'm still in my underwear too. It feels strange to remember what we did hours ago and still be even partially dressed together, but I'm grateful at the same time. I'm not ready to be naked in the dark. With her, I mean. "You enjoyed being with friends and having a good time."

"Yeah, but I was barely making it through my classes. Cs get degrees," she says with a wry tone. "Except that didn't really go over well with my family. We're fourth generation American, but Mom still put lots of emphasis on grades. And, like, if I were in a Lifetime movie, I'd have made some miraculous turnaround after Xue died, and it would all be this big lesson about living to my fullest potential. Mom never said it, but I know she thought maybe I'd go into pre-med also."

"Maternal expectations can be rough. My mom's coped okay, but the biggest problem she's had is me living so far away. She's always pictured me living in Idaho. All the generations nearby, you know?" I roll over and click on my bedside lamp. The shade makes for a diffused yellow glow over Cai and me. "You're really pretty."

"Thanks." Her hair is a black river around her shoulders and over her breasts. Both her knees are bent, casting shadow over her panties. I'm drawn to the hard line between her ribs and the slide down to her stomach.

I didn't take the time last night to really look at Cai's tattoos. They're almost overwhelming in a mix of dark and color. I spread my hand over the soft skin beneath her shallow navel. On the left is a grinning skull in dark colors. A fine spider web drapes around it and spills across her lower stomach. It's grim but so perfectly crafted that it's hard not to admire the delicate lines and gradient shadows. "When did you get this one?"

"About . . . four years ago? I think. A friend of mine did it. Brooke was in training, and she needed to give out some ink."

Even though I know better by now, I'm still a little surprised to touch the skull and not be able to feel anything but Cai's silky skin. The texture is so intricate that it should feel rough like bone would. But it's a part of Cai. "I'd be really nervous about getting a permanent tattoo from someone who was still in training."

"We all have to learn sometime." She points to the front of one of her thighs, which is covered with a portrait of an elephant in an intricately designed frame. "I did this one."

"Upside down?" I twist around on the bed so that I'm facing it properly. I tug at her knee in order to make her lay her legs flat. "You did this upside down?"

"Yeah. I had time and needed to practice." She pushes up onto her elbows. "Check out the bottom-right corner. I really fucked that up."

Once I zero in, I think I see what she's talking about. "Where the lines go together?"

"Yeah. Still annoyed about that. But it's like fifteen years old and still hanging in there, so I guess I did okay."

"That's an understatement." The elephant is staring straight out from the portrait with a lifted trunk. Her eyes are weary. "She's so stately. She's seen a lot. Run from poachers. But maybe she's still trying to live the life she wants to."

I look up and realize Cai's watching me instead of looking at her tattoo. Because duh, she's been living with it for years. There's nothing new in this art that she carries with her. I still admire mine daily. I can't imagine it becoming a forgotten part of my existence.

I think I'm blushing. The tips of my ears tingle. "Is that stupid?"

"No." She shakes her head, still watching me the whole time. "Not stupid."

"But totally over the top. Sorry."

"I like knowing what you're thinking. Don't apologize." She catches my hand and pulls on it, and I do that stupid thing again where I flinch and yank away. I smile and immediately put my hand on her stomach, but I don't think she's buying it.

I'm such an idiot. My insides are shaking. I hold my hand where it is, hoping she can't tell. "Okay," I say blithely, as if I didn't just show off my damages. "I'll give you all my weird brain dumps. No problem."

Her eyes are narrowed. She sees right through me. "What just happened?"

"I don't know what you mean."

There's a long, slow beat of air that can't find its way into my lungs. She covers my hand with hers. Our eyes are locked. It's a screwed-up game. Her fingers wrap around mine. I'm still fine.

She tugs.

I yank backward hard enough that my butt skips four inches across the bed. I drag my legs up so that I'm a knot. "What the fuck?"

"Are you okay?"

"I'd be fine if you weren't trying to haul me around." I cross my legs over my chest. "I think you should go."

"I think we need to talk about this."

I jump off the bed and grab a pair of pajama pants from an open box full of clothes. "There's nothing to talk about. I don't like being shoved around."

She pushes up to a seated position on the edge of the bed. She's naked but for her panties. I'm rapidly getting dressed. I can see the death spiral, and I can't shove my foot in my mouth fast enough.

"I'm sorry," she says. She's so calm, so rational, as if she's intentionally trying not to let the situation escalate. So naturally that only makes me feel even more out of control. "I'm just trying to figure out what's going on here."

"Nothing. Like I said."

"I'm not going to push," she says. "I hope you know that you can tell me anything."

She stands and comes closer to me. Her hands lift as if she's going to soothe a wild animal. I think that makes me the animal in this situation. This has gotten completely out of control. I reach out and grab her, lacing her fingers through mine. It's easier to do than I would have thought. My shoulders unlock enough to relax into a straight line.

"There's nothing to tell. Really. I don't know why I freaked out." I put a smile on my face. "I'm tired and it's late and I have to get up so early. Plus the kids take so much out of me. I'm being weird, and I really didn't mean to."

I hold my breath and my smile. *Don't ask, don't ask*, chants through my head. What we did together earlier in the night was so good. I don't want anything about Jody tainting the memory of being on my knees in front of Cai.

Besides, there really *isn't* anything wrong. I'm overly sensitive. That final night was the crashing end of a relationship that had never been healthy. It wasn't worth this response. Even my brain is blowing it out of proportion. There's no way I could explain this to Cai and sound anything less than crazy. I don't want to talk about it.

She squeezes my fingers and moves close enough that she's inside my space. Our hands are at our hips. "Are you sure?"

"Yeah. Totally. It's fine. I'm fine." If I say it enough times, maybe it'll be true.

"Do you want me to go?" One of her nipples is playing peekaboo from behind the curtain of her hair. She's so confident in herself. Nothing about her seems to faze her. Her tattoos are impenetrable armor.

"It might be for the best. I have to be up in only three hours." I desperately want her to go, and I badly want her to stay at the same time. I don't know how to sort out my own head. "Work tomorrow . . ."

"Yeah. I get it." She cups the side of my face in one hand. Her touch is soft. I lean into it and let my eyes close. "Just . . . tell me if you need something. I'll give it to you if I can."

chapter

Fifteen

Tansy

"Why are you still at the school?"
I'm twenty-five minutes into a conversation with my mom when she drops the question. There's a hundred things I could be doing, but Mom and I have been building a new relationship over the past couple of months. I didn't talk to her much when I was with Jody. It was hard to have a conversation without Jody needing something, or asking questions while I was still on the phone, or jumping into the topic and insisting I put it on speakerphone. I hadn't noticed how short my conversations with my mom had become until it was too late.

I'm flat on my back on the rug in our library nook, my feet up on a padded bench that I usually use when I'm reading to the kids. On the wall above me are the natural disaster projects they turned in last week. Corbyn has a really nice eye for emotion in her drawings. The fear on the faces of the earthquake victims is surprisingly real. I guess that's what Sunday afternoon drawing classes with a Cal Arts student will do for you.

"I had a lot of grading to get done," I tell Mom.

"Couldn't you take it home?"

"It's not exactly cozy there. I haven't really unpacked." I sigh. "Honestly, I haven't unpacked at all."

There's something clattering on the other end. Mom's making dinner. "You've been in that apartment for two months. You know what I say. A tidy room . . ."

111

"Makes for a tidy brain. Yes, Mommy," I tease. "I heard that a thousand times when I was a kid."

"I'm going to send your brother out there."

"Mom, no!" I sit up in a panic. "What?"

"He's bouncing around the house like a bum ever since he got laid off at the factory. He needs something to do." She's got that note of determination in her voice. "He'll come unpack for you."

"That's really not necessary."

"It'll be good for you and good for him."

"Mom, you can't." I rub my forehead. It's not that I suddenly have a headache, but I can feel the pressure of my brains trying to scramble out of my head because I can't figure out how to solve this. "Justin's got a life. He's not your proxy to send off."

"Not much of a life, he doesn't." She makes a tsking sound. "That Johnson girl dumped him, and I can hardly blame her. He was at the bar flirting with Rebecca Wilkins. You know her. She was a year behind you."

Life in a small town is such a weird little dance. There are certain things that are wholly public and other parts that are never talked about. "Is there anything you don't know about his life?"

She gives a tuneless hum as she thinks about it. "I don't think so? Oh! I don't know what kind of porn he likes, thank goodness. But I swear to god that's about it. I need a break from him, Tansy. I haven't had a quiet dinner with your father since Justin moved back in."

"So that's what this is about. Not me unpacking."

"Do your mom a favor." Water's running. I wonder if she's making pasties. Probably not. Too much work for an average weekday. She'd save that for Sundays, when Nanna comes over for what's left of family dinners. I miss those. "I need to get laid."

"Oh my god, Mom," I shout. I sound like a humiliated teenager, and I don't care in the least. "Don't do that to me!"

"I'm just trying to build honesty," she says, but she's laughing too. "Transparency is important in relationships."

"I hate you."

"So I can send Justin?"

"Don't you dare." She can't see it, but I'm wagging a finger. "How about I come visit instead?"

"How does that solve my problem? That's even more people in my house."

"Don't you want to see me?" Mostly, I want her to stop talking about her sex life. Forever. "I'll bring a friend. She'd like hunting, I think."

"A friend?" It's very much like Mom for her to narrow in on that part. "Like a friend-friend? You're not already dating, are you?"

"No," I say, because I don't really know what it is that Cai and I do. We've seen each other a couple more times, but we haven't had sex again. Some make-outs, but not sex. Part of me agonizes about having freaked Cai out, but another part of me has enjoyed the slow burn. Things aren't as heavy as my relationship with Jody, and I can't help but feel like that alone keeps it more casual. Being with someone is supposed to be work, and with Cai it's just fun. No matter if we're playing PS4 games or hunting for the best taco truck, life is good.

"We talked about you having some time to just be yourself."

"Yeah, this is fine. It's no big deal. She's my tattoo artist."

"Your tattoo *what?*" She's practically screeching.

Bingo. That got her off the trail. "Yeah, it's on my calf and it's really pretty. You'll love it. I'm going to check in with Cai—that's her name—and see if she can get off work around my October break."

Because the children attending the academy are the offspring of the rich and entitled, they can't go an entire month of school without having at least a four-day weekend. As a result, we have a random vacation break in October. I'm definitely not complaining. It's the perfect time for hunting white-tailed deer in Idaho.

"You're going to come visit?" Mom's getting excited now that the idea is sinking in. "How long can you stay?"

"I can probably stay the whole week. I'll see if Cai wants to just come up for part of it, or if she has the time off or something. I don't know if she exactly gets vacation hours." Probably not, now that I think about it.

"This will be wonderful! I'll call your nanna. She's missed you so much."

"I know."

It's been four years since I've been home. Jody saw to that. It was never that she said no, we couldn't go visit, but she made it so very,

very hard. I managed to talk her into a trip for Christmas our second year in college. She picked a fight with me the night before. I think it was about taking the trash out—I was nagging her by reminding her, even though the can was literally overflowing and I had nowhere to dump the coffee grounds. She slept on the couch that night and ignored me when I woke her up to go to the airport. Flat out ignored me and pretended to sleep.

It's humiliating to remember the way I begged her to come to the airport and how I apologized for asking her to take the trash out. I couldn't imagine showing up in Boise with an unused ticket and having to explain why my oh-so-wonderful girlfriend decided to bail at the last minute.

Then she made it harder and harder for Mom to visit me.

I cried alone in the bathroom when Mom and Dad quietly sent back their RSVP card marked *not attending*.

God, I had no damn spine.

"This'll be great," I find myself saying, and I mean it. This isn't just about keeping Mom from sending Justin to do my unpacking. I *want* to go visit now. I need to smell the mountains. With or without Cai, for that matter. If I show up alone, that is one hundred percent A-okay with me now. "See if Uncle Theo can come too."

"Sure! Of course!" Mom's bubbling over. "You go buy tickets. I've got to make calls. We'll go shopping too."

"Oh, no way. You're not getting me into Sam's Buckle Emporium." I laugh.

"They have some cute shirts! I need you to tell me how to wear skinny jeans."

"You put one leg in, then the other, and then you pull them up over your butt."

"You're a smart butt." There's a pause, and I can imagine Mom smiling at me. "I've missed you, sugar."

There's a lump in my throat that burns the back of my nose when I try to swallow. "I've missed you too. This is going to be a good trip. I can already tell."

Sixteen

CAI

I wonder if Tansy has any idea how crazy she is. I mean, in a cute way for sure, but she has definitely rounded the bend. "A vacation together?"

"Yeah. Well, sort of. I've got the time off and I want to go home. You mentioned you wanted to try shooting. We can even go hunting if you want. Plus Justin has a couple four-wheelers."

Three weeks ago, I left this woman's apartment in the middle of the night and wasn't sure if I was ever going to hear from her again. I looked up at the glow from her window and honestly expected the light to snap off and that to be the end of it. I was surprised enough when she texted me the next day. Even a little more surprised when we made it to a few dates.

Now I'm sitting at her counter, watching her buzz around her kitchen as she cooks dinner and invites me to visit her family.

This . . . is strange. "Are you sure about this?"

"I mean, it's up to you if you want to come along or meet me there or anything, but I'm definitely going. I haven't been home in years, and now I can't wait."

"That's really good. You should do what makes you happy." I'm just not convinced that I should be going along. I really do want the chance to try shooting. And I've never been hunting in my life. I'm not sure I could really pull the trigger on an innocent deer, especially for sport, but I've always been an advocate of trying things once. I wouldn't have swum with sharks otherwise.

She has a cutting board and a pile of shallots that she's whipping through with a big knife. She tosses them into a skillet liberally covered with olive oil. "Justin's been staying at home for the past few months, so Mom's kind of going nuts."

"How old is he?"

"Twenty-one. He was working at the plastics factory in the next town, but apparently they've shut down one of their products—you'd have to ask him which one—so there were some layoffs. And he got caught up in them."

"That sucks."

"Definitely." She stops slicing pancetta and pops a cube in her mouth. "Do you think you'd want to come?"

"I'd have to check my schedule," I hedge.

"Sure, of course."

"Thanks for making brunch," I say. I hold my hand out to her. She puts her fingers in mine, and I kiss her knuckles. I've learned my lesson about trying to pull her closer to me though. She has to come on her own.

"Anytime." Her smile is cute.

Hell, all of her is cute. She's wearing capri-length jeans rolled at the bottom and a T-shirt big enough to drape off one shoulder. Her curls have been semicorralled into a high ponytail. She's perky today in a way that I haven't seen before. Her plans to go home are lighting her up from the inside. That alone is the most compelling reason I can think of for going, to be able to see how happy she'll be.

"I wish I could have done dinner, but I have to put some hours in at the shop."

"I get it." She finally drifts closer to me. Her chin lifts. Her lips part the slightest bit. I wonder if she realizes she's offering me her mouth. "I guess I'll have to think of some way to amuse myself tonight."

"Think of me?"

"I do that a lot already."

I stroke the shoulder bared by her shirt. "That's good. I think of you too."

"You do?"

"Mm-hmm." Instead of kissing her mouth, I lower my head and brush a kiss over a constellation of freckles right beneath her collarbone. "I was thinking of these freckles when I was trying to work last night. Do you know how bad it is to be distracted while trying to ink someone?"

"Bad?"

"The worst."

I wonder how long it'll take until she kisses me, if she'll ever be that bold. I don't know that she will. There's a part of her that likes submitting, and more than that, I think she likes being chased. Not chased. *Seduced.* I've been deliberate and patient over the last few times we've seen each other, but I don't think I can wait any longer.

I take her wrist and raise it to my mouth. Her pulse throbs when I open my mouth over her skin. She's racing like a rabbit. I feel like a wolf as I lick and kiss her tender flesh. "Little one?"

"Yes?" Her eyes have gone hazy. Her bottom lip is plump and damp.

"I think the onions are burning."

"Oh!" She dashes away and scrambles to the stove. The wooden spoon scrapes across the bottom of the pan. "Oh no, they are. Darn."

It's the charred smell that gave it away. Kind of appealing on one level, but probably not what Tansy was shooting for. Her expression is pinched and displeased. I put an elbow on the counter and hide my smile behind a cupped hand. She's captivating, especially when she stamps one bare foot.

"Ugh. I'm so annoyed."

"Call them caramelized?" I slide up behind her, wrapping my arms around her waist and propping my chin on her shoulder. The onions are definitely black at the edges, but they're probably salvageable. "I like being able to distract you that much."

She covers my hands with one of her own even as she keeps tending the dish. "You've got a little bit of an ego, don't you?"

"Sometimes." I nip her earlobe. She shivers, which in turn bounces a sudden rush of wanting through me too. "Mostly I like you."

I want a chance to order her around again. Perhaps that's terrible, but I don't really care either. If dominance is a spectrum, I've always been more on the bossy end, but I haven't gone so far as BDSM. With Tansy, I can easily make an exception. There's something about the way she looks at me that I need more of. I want that laser focus and the way it's combined with a need to take care of her.

"I like you too," she says as she tilts her head so I can have easier access. Her ponytail spills over our arms.

I lay a line of kisses up and down her neck. Gentle. Soft. The flutter of my lips over her flawless, pale skin. Her pulse throbs under my mouth. I apply a tiny lick. Skin doesn't taste like that much on its own, not usually. On Tansy, I taste the promise of things to come. It's the heady flavor of possibility.

"Why don't you turn that off?" I suggest gently.

Her hand immediately goes to the stove's control, but then she hovers over it. "Are you sure? You're not hungry?"

"We can order delivery later if you need it."

Her skin is warm and edging toward hot as I kiss and lick her. My hands roam over her curves and valleys wherever I like. Holding her hips, I push her to the side, away from the stove. One by one I take her hands and lay them flat on the edge of the travertine counter.

"Don't move," I order her.

"Okay." Her throat constricts on a compulsive swallow. She dips her head enough that her ponytail falls between her face and me and hides her. I push it away. I want to see everything I do reflected in her expressions. With Tansy, there's no second that's wasted.

I stand behind her, my front plastered against her back. My nipples are hard with desire and my pussy is starting to feel needy. Even the abrasion of my shirt against my tits helps me along. "What would you do if I walked away right now?"

"Cry?" she offers helplessly. It's a joke, but I think it's not at the same time. She leans back on her heels, obeying my order but seeking more attention from me. "I don't think I'd like to be left alone. I know I wouldn't."

"But you do like it when I order you around."

"I do."

"And if I make you into my personal play toy?"

"I'd be the best toy I could be." She slides me a sideways glance out of the corner of her eyes. "Can I volunteer for sex toy duty in particular? I liked making you feel good."

I groan, low and absolutely unintentionally. "You're wicked."

"I am, aren't I?" Her grin sparks. "You make me wicked, I think."

I'm petting her all over. My hands on her stomach, on her hips, riding between her legs. Ribs and back and pushing under the hem of her shirt. I pop open the button of her jeans and immediately shove between panties and rough pants to get a handful of the sweet curve of her ass. "Sweet, sweet girl."

"Take care of me? You'll treat me right. Please?"

I haven't tasted her yet. I don't think I can go a moment longer without knowing what she'll feel like coming on my face. "Go to the couch."

"Yes, ma'am," she says, and I shudder with both the words and the way she looks saying them. She knows it's a moment, a big deal, a thing that there's no stepping back from. She looks up at me from under her lashes.

She sashays toward her sectional with her ass swaying. The jeans are loose around her hips but still holding on. Her feet are bare and pale in contrast to the maple floors. When she gets to the dark-blue couch, she immediately strikes the same pose that she'd been in against the counter—hands spread on the back of the couch and leaning over.

"Jesus Christ, little one."

"Is this bad?" She looks back at me over her shoulder, eyes wide. I can't tell if she's worried or if she's teasing me.

"Only in the way that it's so good, it's bad." I stay far enough away that I can't touch yet. I want to take in the whole picture. "You should see how goddamned good your ass looks. You're so sexy."

She hides her face against her shoulder. "I've never really thought of myself as sexy. I'm a girl-next-door type."

"You are incredibly sexy. Fucking hell, you so are."

She's bent over, her ass cocked out enough that her shirt pools in the small of her back. The silky material slides over her skin when I push it up. Her bra is pale peach this time. When I tug her jeans down, I discover gauzy panties to match. She's patient. Incredibly so. She doesn't even step out of her jeans until I nudge her one foot at a time and pull them away.

I set her feet shoulder-width apart. Her turn on has a wild, musky scent. The center of her panties has a wet circle. I press a single fingertip to the exact middle of it. She lets out a quiet "Oh!"

"Do you want my mouth?"

"Yes, please."

"Do you think you deserve it?"

She freezes, the little motions of her hands and feet and the way her hips were moving with need all stopping. "I—I don't know?"

"Have you been a good girl lately?"

"Yes." She flashes me a naughty smile, and her hips start shifting again. It's like she's turned on a switch and gotten into the sense of the game. "I've done all my chores, and I'm completely up-to-date on my homework."

We're on the same wavelength. A dirty, filthy game that I never would have thought to ask for, but now that we've fallen into it, I feel the pull deep in my psyche. "What about your essay?"

"Oh, no," she says in a faux-dismayed voice. "I didn't know I had an essay."

I'm torn between wanting to laugh my ass off and wanting to fuck this girl silly. It takes me a moment to be able to give her a *tsk-tsk*. "What are we going to do about you?"

"Punish me?" she asks, wholly eager and excited. She bounces on her toes, which makes her calves flex. I did a damn good job on that tattoo of hers. I could kiss it for bringing this minx into my life. "Punishment with oral sex, yup. I think that's where we need to go with that."

I lose the battle and laugh. "That doesn't sound like it's going to inspire discipline in you."

"Maybe it depends how good you are?" She giggles. "I only learn lessons if the oral sex is really, really good."

"I don't think that's how it works."

She wags her butt. "We can try it and see?"

When I started this game, I had some half-formed idea of spanking her, but I don't think that's going to serve. Not this time. I sit myself down on the couch and lean against the cushions. "Go stand in the corner."

"What?" She gawps at me, her jaw so wide that I see teeth and tongue.

I cross my arms over my chest and fold an ankle over my knee. Very much the displeased-professor sort of pose. "You heard me, little one. You're being cheeky. You need a time out."

"You can't be serious." Her eyes are so wide, it's almost comical. The pretty hazel is completely ringed by white. I can't help but notice that her breathing is getting even faster and she hasn't moved from her subservient position bent over the couch. With me sitting next to her, there's absolutely nothing keeping her in place but her own desire.

This whim is rapidly turning into a hard-core fetish. I am so fucking turned on. Everything inside me has hit a level of intense calm that I haven't felt before. I lift a single eyebrow. "Go. Stand in the corner."

chapter

Seventeen

TANSY

"*W*hat happens if I don't do it?"

"I leave." Cai points at my front door. Her motorcycle waits outside. "I'll walk away."

She's serious. I think she is, at least? This is all new to me. I'm tempted to break character even further and ask if it's new to her as well. But I don't think we could get back to this place of play again so easily if I ask.

I do have to admit that I'm into this. A little weirded out, maybe, but also definitely into it. I take one hand off the back of the couch at a time and stand, watching Cai while I do. Like maybe she's going to back down?

She doesn't. Her expression is stern, and even her clothes are appropriate to the situation. She's wearing trousers and a short-sleeved button-down with a vest over it. The dark spill of her hair over her shoulder provides delicious contrast. Her tie has lemon-yellow stripes. I love the rough and tumble of her tattooed arms. She's a dyke in the best sense, and I love it.

I'm going to die of how perfect this all is.

I pad quietly over to the corner of the living room. There's not even any art on the wall, since I haven't hecking unpacked. I have to stand next to a waist-high stack of brown boxes.

I clasp my hands behind my butt and turn my toes toward each other for an extra sense of playing-along-ness. This is stupid. This is ridiculously hot. I don't know why. I don't even know if I want to look at my whys. Maybe not now, at least.

How long is she going to leave me here? I can't ask. I know automatically that it goes against the rules of this game.

I wonder what she'd do if I put my hand in my panties and started rubbing. Maybe then I'd get the kind of punishment I expected.

I love having the tables turned on me. She's keeping me on my toes, which is a beautiful counterpoint to the places my head can go sometimes.

I need to come. More than want, even. It's bone-deep in a way that has even my fingertips tingling. I can't remember ever feeling like this before.

My hands slide from behind my butt to in front of my waist. I lock them tight, palm to palm, as if that'll give me the strength to hold down this wave of horniness. Ugh, I don't even like that word, but I can't think of anything else that so completely covers how I feel. I want to bang Cai like a storm door in a breeze, and without the opportunity to do so, I'm tempted to rub myself on the stack of boxes next to me like a cat in heat.

I slip my hands down and press the base of my palms above my clit. It feels so good, but it's not enough either. I let go, then do it again. Holy crud, it won't take long at all until I can come this way.

"Put your hands behind your back."

I jolt, lifting up on my toes, my knees turning inward.

"I'm sorry," I say automatically, but oh my gosh, I don't want to do it either. My arms are creaky with resistance. I could cry. "Please, Cai. I'm sorry, I won't do it again. I need you."

"How bad do you want to come?"

"It's everything. I need it so badly."

"Crawl to me."

I can't help it; I half turn to look at her. She's sitting on the couch, both arms hooked wide over the back and her knees splayed. Her eyebrows are lifted in challenge, and her smile is coolly erotic. She is one hundred percent bad bitch. I shudder. "What?"

"Crawl to me, kiss my boots, and beg me to fuck you."

This is kind of one of the weirdest feelings in the world. I want to hate this more than I do. Like, part of me is sitting back thinking, *Naw, this ain't gonna happen*, while the rest of me is absolutely barking dying for it. I let that part win.

I drop to my hands and knees.

It's easy to crawl. I never would have expected that, but it is. I'm practically floating. Every bit of me is high as a kite even as I can hardly get any lower. It's the way she's staring at me. I can't breathe. It's all so much. There's so much wetness coming from me that the tops of my thighs slide with it.

When I get to Cai, I kneel at her feet with my ass in the air and my shoulders low. I curl both hands around her black boot and kiss the polished toe. It's slick and hard under my lips. "Daddy, please. Won't you make your girl feel good? I need it. I need to come. I need *you* to make me come."

Her groan is deliciously layered with angst and want. "Fuck, little one. You're seriously good at that."

"Will you make me feel nice, Daddy?"

"Up here," she says in a gruff order even as she grabs my shoulders and manhandles me into lying flat on the couch.

I giggle, but I'm also twisting inside every cell I have. I like the way she's holding me. So firm and confident. There's no worry that maybe she doesn't want me, or want to play like this. She's in it. I'm in it. Even the soft couch fabric is too much for how sensitive I am. I arch my back. "Suck my breasts? Can you please?"

"You're awfully bossy for a little girl," Cai teases. Her hand cups me, one thumb softly rubbing my nipple—and then not so softly when she catches it between thumb and finger and twists.

I practically launch off the couch, but I'm just trying to get more and more. It's pain mixed with sweet. I can't put the feeling into words, and all I know is that if it ends, I may cry.

Then Cai shoves one of my legs up and buries her face in my panties, and I scream instead. The silky material is so wet that it's hardly there. Cai's tongue is enough to light me on fire. I'm dying in the best way.

She grabs the gusset of my undies and yanks. The lace panels at my hip bones pop and rip. Cai throws the panties over her shoulder and brings every bit of her energy to bear on me.

I shove both hands to my mouth. There's pain when my palms grind my lips into my teeth. I don't care. I don't care at all, because Cai's licking me and eating me.

I can't tell the separate things she's doing. It's all blended together. My clit throbs with her attention, but none of the rest of me is hungry either. She's mouth fucking me. This is no passive act the way I did for her the other day. It's a gift, but it's also a warning.

This is a woman who fucks. Not making love or coming together or any of those things I've called it before.

She is fucking me.

And, god, do I love it.

My orgasm comes between one breath and the next. There's no windup, no warning beyond how expertly she's working me. One second I'm turned on and going nuts but not quite there, and the next second I'm shaking apart. The feelings rock from my clit to my empty sheathe and sneak up to snatch me by the throat. I don't know what I say. They're just words that are being ripped from the very core of me, the parts that Cai is laying waste to.

And she's not letting up. She backs off only enough for me to remember how to breathe, and then her lips and tongue are back to work. She sucks my flesh farther into her mouth than I would have thought possible. Her explorations know no bounds, and she even delves between my cheeks to lick and probe the dark star there. I squirm at first, but as soon as the hot sensation of steamy pressure gets past my surprise, I'm squirming for an entirely different reason.

It takes me far longer to get to my second orgasm, but Cai never betrays the slightest shred of impatience. Gosh, she never even falters in her enthusiasm. It's all full throttle, and the way she licks me and sucks me and nibbles is exactly what I need. I ride the swollen, heart-thumping pleasure up and up and up until I practically float away. This come seems to start in my chest, with great, huge gasps. My stomach clenches, and then everything is free and I'm loose on a storm of sensation. I break apart all the way down to my toes.

I come screaming Cai's name.

chapter

Eighteen

CAI

We're playing footsie, except with both hands and feet. We're spooned on the couch and Tansy's nakedness is curled up against my side. She stacks her toes on top of mine and then lines up the base of her palm to measure against mine. "You have bigger hands than me."

"I'm taller than you. Makes sense." I twine our fingers and lift the combined hands. She comes with me as easily as if I were leading her in a kids game. "I kept growing after twelve."

"Twelve! I don't look like a tween."

"You certainly don't," I say with an intentional leer at her perfect, perky tits. I cup one and duck to kiss the tip. I add a bit of tongue for good measure.

She shivers and shoves her free hand through my hair. Even when she's greedy, she's delicate, and her weight is barely noticeable. "Besides. When I was twelve, you were twenty-six. That's creepy."

"Ew!" I bolt upright. "What the hell?"

She smirks, her mouth turned up in the most adorable tease. She's looking at me from under her lashes, and she leans back against the ample couch cushions, seeming more like the Queen of Sheba than the nymph she normally reminds me of. Watching her grow into herself is starting to blow my mind, bit by bit. She's fascinating. "Do the math, sweetie."

I pause. Compare my birth date to hers. "That's a little much."

"I promise I wouldn't have hit on you."

"You wouldn't have been capable of it. Even if you thought you were trying." I open my arms, and she returns to leaning into me. "I can't picture twelve-year-old Tansy in Idaho."

"I probably looked a lot like twelve-year-olds anywhere. Except less eyelashes. Curse of being a true redhead. My lashes were practically invisible until I learned how to use mascara without poking myself in the eyeballs."

I laugh, then tilt her chin toward the ceiling. "Yup, wearing it now, aren't you?"

"Always. I've been thinking about getting lash extensions." She grins, but I think she's also watching my reaction carefully.

"That's a thing?"

"Yeah. They're glued in one by one." She looks down at our joined hands and draws a pattern across my palm. "Probably a waste of money."

"If you're expecting me to freak out, it's not going to happen. Go be a girly girl. I think it's sexy as fuck." I'm rewarded with a pink flush across the tops of her cheeks and down her throat. She curls up even closer to my side, nuzzling her way under one of my arms. I squeeze her shoulders. "I put ink in people's skin for a living. If that's not a waste of money, some eyelashes sure aren't."

"How did you get into tattoos? As a job?"

"By getting into them being on my body first." I push up the sleeve of my T-shirt. It's the original Barbie doll in the black-and-white-striped swimsuit. The brunette version instead of the blonde though. "This was my first. A memorial for my sister."

She touches the curve of Barbie's hip, and I'm the one who catches the sensation. "She liked dolls?"

"Always swore that the very first thing she got with a physician's paycheck was going to be a 1959. She already knew a vintage dealer she trusted who she was going to buy from."

"Why Barbie?"

"Living the American dream." I sigh. "So then I got a fenghuang on my back for my heritage, and then a couple others. I didn't really want to leave the shops. I liked how laid-back everyone seemed. I mean, I found out eventually that was bullshit."

Tansy pushes her hair back from her face so that she can lean on my shoulder. Her jaw cracks on a huge yawn. "What do you mean?"

"We're all just as crazy or driven or whatever as picket fence America in our own way." I like her curls. Petting them is like plunging my hand into a cloud. "Skylar, who runs the shop? She's got too many balls in the air. She's going to explode someday. We each have our secrets."

"And yours is that you like BDSM?"

"Not really."

She freezes like a trapped rabbit. I think even the tip of her nose twitches. "Does that mean you don't like . . . what we did?"

There's no way I'm letting this go by without explanation. I scoop her up and arrange her so that she's sitting in my lap. Her butt is nestled across my thighs, and I hook an arm around her bent knees. "That is not what I said at all. I've liked it a fuck of a lot."

That gets a giggle out of her, but she's still avoiding my gaze. She twiddles with the top button of my vest instead. "'A fuck of a lot' seems like plenty."

"A mega fuck-ton?"

"That's good with me." She glances up at me from under those mascara-ed lashes. "So it's good with you?"

"Yeah. You can say that again."

"But you haven't done it before?" If she keeps at that button the way she is, twisting it back and forth, it's going to pop off. I don't try to stop her. "Because it seemed like you knew what you were doing."

"I'm not going to lie and say I'm a saint or anything." I push the ends of her red curls back over her shoulder. She's dotted with orange freckles. "I've played in dungeons before. Sometimes I've bottomed."

"What?" She jerks her head up on a little squeak. "That's not right."

I chuckle and pull her closer. She smells like sugar and a heavy dose of girl juices. "It was right for the moment. It wouldn't be right with you."

"I'm the first one you've . . . ordered around?"

"Yeah."

"Why?"

I take my time thinking about it, remembering how she'd locked up that first time. The way she'd looked at me when I was in the shower and she knelt before me. The hard shot of pleasure that I'd felt at the sight. "It seemed like what we both needed."

She keeps her head bent. Her jaw slides against my collarbone, but she doesn't end up saying anything for a long moment. "I like it. But I worry that means there's something wrong with me. After . . . after the way things used to be, shouldn't I want to be calling the shots and be the one who starts everything? I should be bar hopping and taking home whoever I feel like. That's the way it's supposed to be."

I wonder about the spaces between Tansy's words sometimes. I don't know what she means about 'the way things used to be' and I want to know in order to shore up her defenses. But I don't think I can ask. Not now. I take what she's offered me and no more. "Whatever you're doing is the way it's supposed to be. No matter if that was standing on street corners wearing a clown costume and turning somersaults."

"Clowns are creepy."

"Pink flamingo costume."

"Much better." She kisses the side of my neck in the soft space underneath my jaw. "Though I don't think a flamingo would survive a somersault."

"Might be worth watching."

I brush my mouth over hers. She's sweet as sin and twice as tempting. I can't seem to go very long without having my hands all over her. Her neck tilts, and it's like I have every bit of her open to me. She'd give me anything.

It's heady and distracting and almost overwhelming. I want to take and take without giving. I teeter on the edge between greediness and needing to nurture her. It's different from moment to moment. I wonder if that's what makes her different.

I wonder if I'll ever tell her that she's different.

chapter

TANSY

The day before I leave for Idaho flies by. It seems like I blink and I'm standing outside of the academy, waving at Mink's Lexus. The red Lexus as opposed to the blue one. October in California doesn't have the same feeling that it does back home. The sun's warmth lies on my shoulders until I duck under the shade of the portico. I'm wearing capris and a sleeveless silk top, but it's still hot as hell and pushing ninety degrees. A bead of sweat rolls down the center of my back. I can't wait to go home.

I wish I could wear sunglasses, but it's frowned on at arrivals and departures. Parents like the emotional connection of being able to see our eyes. They want to be able to see our deference.

"I am going to melt." Imogene flaps a hand at herself. "I'm from freaking Toronto. I'm not built for this heat."

I do a little dance. "Gonna be much cooler in Idaho."

"Shove it, woman. Stop bragging."

My stomach does a flip, I do an instant replay of what I just said and wonder if I went too far, but then I decide that nope, I'm going further. "Boots and pumpkin spice and falling leaves! Actual autumn. It's a thing."

"Not in Southern California, it's not." She laughs and opens the door to the building for me. "I hate fall. It means winter's coming."

"I guess there's a reason you moved here?"

She leans against the wall beside her classroom. Over her shoulder is a montage of her class's photographs from their monthly trip to the

Los Angeles County Museum of Art. They're working on an in-depth exploration of multisensory art. "There's a load of reasons, but yeah, the weather is one of them. I hate the snow."

"I kind of miss it." I sigh. "Okay, I really miss it. I used to ski!"

Imogene's perfectly groomed brows lift. "I don't think I can picture you in a snow suit."

"I loved it. And I didn't mind the short days, and I loved being inside and having hot cocoa afterwards."

She grins. "Now that, I can imagine."

"I don't know, maybe I'm romanticizing it." I lean against the wall beside her, but I fail at cool points and have to pull my hair away from construction paper tesseracts. "It's been forever since I've been home, and actually living in a place like that is so different."

"I always hated the way everything was gray by January."

"Yeah, the road salt is nasty."

She shudders and wrinkles her nose. "It'd be fine if it were just the roads. But it's all over the sidewalks and tracks in your house and corrodes your car. I am so glad to be done with that shit."

"I miss it." I sigh again and my shoulders drop. "And it sounds so far away."

"Then go home." She says it so casually, so easily. As if it wouldn't be the biggest upheaval of my life.

No, wait, I think that was maybe leaving Jody at the altar. That was probably bigger. "I can't."

"Sure you can. Working here will give you a killer résumé. You're single. You can go wherever you want."

I blush. It's like a firecracker that goes off in my cheeks and lights me on fire. I keep my gaze carefully trained on the poster on the other side of the hallway for our school concert and hope Imogene doesn't have great peripheral vision. But naturally she does.

"You *are* single, aren't you?" She stands straight and gawps at me. The goddess braids curved around the top of her head, combined with her height, make her a little intimidating. "Tell me you did *not* take Jody back."

"No! God, no." I jolt at the sudden terror that even the thought of having Jody back in my life brings. My palms sweat and my heart rate hits a speed that's totally insane. "Never. I wouldn't anyways, but it's not like she's even been trying either. We're so done."

"Thank you, my sweet Baby Jesus." She presses her palms together as if it's a real prayer. Maybe it is. "Who you got them thoughts about, then, huh?"

"I guess you won't believe me if I say Angelina Jolie?"

"Her too, I bet, but I want the real-deal info." She points at her classroom. "Come in for tea."

I shake my head. "Can't. I have to go home and pack. My flight's at six tomorrow morning, and then I have a connection too. Nothing flies straight through to Idaho."

Besides, I have no real idea what I'd say about Cai. We're not a long-term, forever kind of thing, and yet she's meeting me at home in three days. What do you call that? More than friends with benefits. Less than a relationship. The exact person I needed at the right moment in my life?

Words are hard.

Imogene is exasperated with me, but I think it's in a gentle friendship kind of way. I hope. "At least tell me if I know her."

"You don't. I promise."

She narrows her eyes and points at me as if she's had a huge revelation. "The cat basket! With the toys."

"Gyoza likes her," I say on a laugh. "A lot."

"She must be good people."

"I think so." It's the perfect moment to say something about hoping my mom thinks so too, but I've kept it such a secret that Cai will be in Idaho that I don't know how to start now. Maybe it's just something Imogene doesn't need to know. After all, I can barely stand to look sideways at the situation myself. Explaining to my mom was one of the weirdest conversations of my life, but I managed.

"You make sure she treats you right, sugar. If she doesn't, she's going to have to answer to me. I'm not keeping my mouth shut this time."

Imogene holds her arms out for a hug, and I steel myself enough to step into it. She smells like cocoa for some reason. It's awkward at first. I'm stiff. It's hard to be touched still. But then she pats my back and lets go and my feel-good feelings come in the wake of freedom. I know I'm backward. Hugs aren't supposed to only be pleasant afterward, but in the middle I'm waiting for something bad to happen. It's like I can only process little pieces at a time.

I don't like to look inward at myself. It's broken in there, filled with shards of glass that hurt to turn over. I'll start bleeding all over the painted wood floors. The cheery blue and gold diamonds wouldn't do very well with pools of crimson. Not to mention it'd be hard to explain to the janitorial staff.

I am nothing if not considerate.

"Thanks. I'll be sure to warn her." I make myself smile at my friend even though it's still hard to believe that I've had friends all along.

Now it's time to go remind myself that I've always had my family too.

✦✦✦✦✦✦

"Oh my god, Mom. No! I'm going to freaking choke you!"

She is absolutely, gleefully unrepentant. An outright cackle comes out of her. "Welcome home, baby!"

Our driveway is filled with people. Absolutely packed. Mom has to park her Jeep on the curb. There are balloons and ribbons and my high school girlfriend. Beth holds a poster board sign reading, *Welcome Home!* over her head and waves it back and forth. Dad is at the front of the crowd, standing with his hands fisted on his hips and his feet spread in the *I belong in my world* pose that he's always had. Nanna waves manically. She's wearing a bright-blue track suit.

I'm laughing and dying at the same time. "This is insane."

"Everyone was so happy when I told them you were coming back."

"It's not like I've been to war or something!" I unbuckle, but I can't look away from the craziness in front of me either.

"You've been in California. For *years*. It's practically the same thing." Mom sniffs the way she always does when she talks about California. It's a reflex, the same exact thing that Grandpa Harold did before he died. But then she pushes a bit of my hair back over my shoulder and pets my head. "We've missed you."

I know she's saying she in particular missed me. When she picked me up at the Idaho Falls airport, I was struck by how much older she looked than I remembered. There are lines at the corners of her eyes and her skin is pale but just a little bit more dull than she should be. I get my curls from her, but hers are now shot through with a pretty solid amount of gray.

"I've missed you too, Mom."

Mom's hug is a safe one even if it's awkward over the center console and stick shift. I have no doubts, no bit of freezing. It's only the burning tears that I have to hold back with a few blinks and a sniffle.

Then I'm out of the car, and Dad is the first one to grab me. He smells like motor oil and his baseball cap is shoved back on his head enough that I can see his hair has receded another few inches. "Muffin!"

"Daddy." I burrow my face against his chest. He's nearly a foot taller than me.

"Your mom made your favorite. Tater tot casserole." He pats my back. "You're lucky. She doesn't make it for me anymore. Says my blood pressure can't take it."

This is my dad. The man who can squeeze me so hard that my ribs hurt a little, but who can only talk about the food that Mom's prepared. I guess he's who I get my difficulties expressing myself from. But not this time. "I'm glad to be home, Daddy."

"Yeah. I know, muffin. I know."

And then he lets me go. I'm pulled into a vortex of family and friends. It's the strangest feeling to know every one of their names. I hadn't realized how isolated California can be. I've been in crowded yoga classes and not even known the instructor's name. But this is one big line of people who wiped my butt and aren't afraid to remind me, or who copied off my test in World History or who I played with in creeks and climbed trees.

At one point I turn around and find Beth, who's grinning at me like a mad hatter. Her hair is cropped super short, and she's wearing a Cabela's T-shirt under an open flannel. She smacks me on the back hard enough that I stumble. "Holy shit, woman! You have no idea how good it is to not be the token lesbian anymore."

"I'm only here for a week," I say and then laugh.

"I'll take what I can get." She gives her sign a wiggle. "You gotta come by the shop."

"Shop?"

"I bought old man Nowacki's garage. I'm the only game in town if your radiator goes out."

"I'll keep it in mind." I grin at her. "We should get coffee."

Her laugh is grand and wide open. "I'm in. We'll go to your grandma's place."

"We can get that booth in the back corner and pretend no one knows what we're talking about."

She leans in and drops her voice as if we're going to share a secret. "Rebecca's ass is still as hot as it's always been. Just sayin'."

"I heard that!" exclaims a deep voice. "And I completely agree."

My brother is even taller than our dad. I have to crane my neck to look at him. "Justin! Get down here and hug me."

And the smart-ass goes to his knees there in the driveway. He throws his arms wide. "There. Is that better?"

"You're still my younger brother, and I still reserve the right to beat you up." Except it pretty much brings his head to my shoulder level, so I hug him. This thing is getting easier each time. "I'll have to jump you when you're not expecting it."

Mom claps and then waves her hands over her head. "Let's take this party inside. Food's in the kitchen, drinks are in the coolers on the back porch. Off we go!"

Justin hops back up to his feet. He and Beth throw their arms around my shoulders and herd me toward the house. Dad grabs my suitcase, but Frank, his best friend of thirty years and a guy who's practically an uncle to me, grabs my tote bag. It's pretty cute to see burly, bearded Frank with a bright-pink shopping tote hooked over one shoulder, but then I let Justin and Beth lead me away into my childhood home.

This feels like more than a visit. The warmth in my chest and my heart says I'm where I'm supposed to be. These are the people who know me and who would have kept me safe from the beginning. Even the crisp air carries a scent of greenery and the smallest hint of wood smoke. Orange leaves crackle underfoot.

I don't regret leaving, but I don't know if I want to go away again. Except Idaho doesn't have Cai.

CAI

*I*nsisted on renting a car and driving up from Idaho Falls on my own. The drive was pretty awesome. I like my personal time, and I'd gotten almost three hours in the car, cranking the stereo, on a drive that's very different than three hours in the car in Southern California. The mountains spoke for themselves. Vibrant colors, twisting roads, and the freedom to smash down the gas pedal as much as I felt like.

If I'm honest, I'm damn lucky I didn't catch myself a speeding ticket, but all's well that ends well.

I also insisted on getting a room at one of three motels in town, but as I pull up to the Seeker Inn, I kind of second-guess that choice. The two-story motel and one-story office are both painted a pinkish orange that might be something like salmon pink. Maybe. If the sun were setting and I squinted a lot.

The parking lot is surprisingly full. I find a spot between a mud-splattered F-150 and a Chevy, and the rental RAV4 that felt fun and roomy when I picked it up at the airport is suddenly dwarfed. I haul my hiking backpack out of the rear and swing it over a shoulder.

I stand inside the door and take the time for a really good look around. The floor is large gray tiles, not the shag orange that the walls would make me expect. Once it all sinks in, I realize the furniture is pretty industry-standard motel stuff. Nubby polyester upholstered chairs flank black metal tables. Through an archway to the right is a breakfast area with small bistro tables made of wrought iron.

There's a check-in desk topped with gray marble that coordinates with the floor tiling, and behind the desk is a young guy with stick-straight, dirty-blonde hair.

Everything is surprisingly up-to-date. Huh. Even the desk clerk is alert and totally on top of his job. He has me checked in less than ten minutes after I walk through the door. I barely have time to text Tansy that I've arrived. I send her my room number once I get that too.

But despite hitting Go on the text literally as I step into the room, I've barely unpacked my T-shirts before I hear a knock. I open the door half expecting the desk clerk or a random stranger, but it's definitely Tansy.

I would know that cloud of curls anywhere. She's got on a pair of faded-out jeans that I don't remember seeing in California. They hang low on her hips, and the Henley she's wearing emphasizes the curves of her body. Damn, she looks good.

"Were you waiting around the corner or something?"

"Nope. I was home. It's a small town. Doesn't take long to get across. Not like San Sebastian. I haven't sat in traffic for days!" She brushes past me and throws herself down on the king-sized bed. "I take it back. I'm glad you got a motel room. This bed is huge."

"Hey." I snap it as crisply as I can manage. "You haven't greeted me properly."

"What?" She sits back up, her eyes wide. The bedspread is dark blue. Her pale skin glows. She looks healthier here. Or maybe it's happier? When I first met Tansy, she had the edge of panic to every word that came out of her mouth. Even though I'm acting firm, that feeling is gone.

"Come kiss me."

A smile blooms across her mouth. She slides off the bed and saunters toward me. The usual sweetness clings to her, but it's mixed with a hint of wood smoke. "That I can do," she purrs.

She leans up on her toes and mates her mouth to mine. Her lips taste like candied apples. We aren't touching anywhere but at our mouths, and it's beautiful and serene.

We've been seeing each other two and three times a week in California, and it has been only three days ahead of me that Tansy arrived in Idaho. How could I have grown to miss her in that time?

It seems like an impossibility, something that's bigger than me and as mysterious as a phantom at the same time. Like a ghost, she's going to slip through my fingers.

That magic quality she has, the ability to keep going despite the fear that I can read on her . . . She's strong in a way I never thought to be. It was the months between Xue disappearing and finding her body that were the worst. The not knowing sank into my bones. The terror was never ending—sometimes I think in a literal way that's still holding on to me.

Tansy has been through hell and come out as startlingly earnest as a grown human can be.

I've never tried to hold on to anyone before. I don't know what to do this time.

She drops down. I smile at her and tap the end of her perky button nose. "Good girl."

Her smile turns into a laugh. "Should I say 'Woof woof'?"

I even feel goofy about her straight, white teeth. Only straight thing I like on her. This is ridiculous. I catch her around the waist. Our curves align. Where her hips go in, mine go out. Her breasts are soft. "I could give puppy play a shot if you really wanted. I don't know that it'd come naturally."

She giggles some more and covers her face with her hands. Splotches of bright red tint the tops of her cheeks and her ears anyway. "No! No, no, I didn't even know that was a thing. Is that a thing? Really?"

"Some people like it." I fold and bury my face in her neck as I make a growling noise. "See? You liked that there."

"It tickled," she exclaims with another round of laughter. "Physiological reactions can't be controlled."

Her arms hook around my neck, and she leans back so that a lot of her body weight dangles. She's trusting me to hold her up.

I won't let her fall.

Even if it scares the shit out of me.

We're supposed to go over and meet her family for dinner, but one more kiss won't kill us, so I take it. Except she melts into my arms like some sort of end-of-the-video-game prize. I claim her mouth and my hand is at her breast before I realize what's going on. I end the kiss and push her back. "Nuh-uh. I am not going to sleep with you right before meeting your dad."

She scoots into my arms again and curls her hands around the bottom hem of my T-shirt. She rubs her knuckles over my bare skin. "Are you sure? Are you really sure?"

"Are you *trying* to get me in trouble?"

"Would you spank me if I said yes?" She's in full minx mode, with that teasing smile on her lips. She wiggles a little bit. "It's not like I had high school boyfriends. The whole rebellion thing passed me by. I think Jody was about as close as I got to it, and she was like a grenade who pulled her own pin. I never really knew when she was going to go off."

"That sounds seriously shitty." The time I met Jody, she was a real peach, and I've guessed she must have been a bitch, but I think this is more than Tansy has ever said about her before. When I take Tansy's hands, they're ice-cold.

She shrugs as if it doesn't matter anymore. I want that to be true, but I wonder how much she's been hurt. Where her wounds end. I'm not a surgeon, but I'm someone who cares about her. Maybe I can help sew her up.

"So now is fun. I kind of want to parade you all around town. Everyone's going to love you."

"I don't know about that," I say as I shake my head. "I'm not exactly small-town material. All the tats."

"Eh." She pets the ink on my arm. "You're not as edgy as you think you are."

"You take that back, or I'll start growling again."

"See?" She hooks a hand around the back of my head and pulls my mouth down to her. "All bark, no bite."

"I'll order you to your knees again."

"Like that's a hardship." She darts her tongue out and licks my bottom lip, then kisses the moisture away. "I ain't afraid of you, lady."

I hug her. I hold her body to mine as tight as I can manage, and she squeezes me back. We're a port in an invisible storm. In my head it's calm. I want her. I want to keep her, this mix of vulnerable and innocent that she has mastered. The pile of her hair covers my face, and I breathe her in.

I'm going to have a life full of Tansy Gavin, and my world is going to be better for it.

"Kneel," I order her.

She sinks gracefully and immediately. Her gaze stays linked to mine. I'll be damned if I'm gonna be the first one to look away.

Her touch skims down my shoulders, over the backs of my wrists, and finds purchase at the front of my jeans. She looks up at me, thumb rubbing the metal button. "May I?"

"May you what?"

Her eyes are luminous against the pale arch of her cheek. The sweep of her lashes has depth it hadn't before. I think she got those lash things she was talking about. The effect is subtle, but it makes her even more beautiful. I have a wood nymph kneeling before me. "May I take your pants down? Please, miss?"

I have to hold back a little smile, because *miss* doesn't seem like a name that fits me in the least. I'm a ballbuster, a broad. *Miss* is for women who attend church or are younger than twenty. That hasn't been me for a long time. "You may unbutton me."

She opens the snap and lowers the zipper—and I snag her hand. "Uh-uh. Naughty little one. I only said you could unbutton, not unzip."

A gasp flies from her parted lips. "You tricked me!"

"Did I? Or did you get greedy and hear what you wanted to hear?"

She drops her gaze, and she's hiding her own teasing smile. There are stars in her eyes. "I got greedy. I like having all of you, mistress."

I laugh, and it's okay because she giggles. "No, I don't think that one works either."

"I need something to call you, don't I?" She speaks so innocently, as if I'm not going to notice the way she's inveigling her hands between the back waistband of my jeans and my panties. She grips my ass and squeezes. Sneaky gropes. I'll let it pass because I like the hungry way she eyes me up. "Your name feels too informal right now. And I like the way you call me 'little one.'"

"Is that what I say? It's fitting." I wrap a lock of her hair around a finger.

She widens her knees and comes closer to me so that they're on either side of my toes. Her cheek lies against my stomach. "It makes me feel good when you use it. Small in a good way."

"Have you been small in a bad way before?" I ask before I think it through.

Her grip on my ass tightens, and she presses her cheek against me. For a moment I think that's going to be all the answer I get. The air in the meager room is still. I can hear my own pulse in my ears. The tiny shuffle of leather against carpet when she shifts one foot.

Then she nods. "I have." Her voice is small to match. "So small I could have disappeared."

We hold each other for a long moment. I may be the one standing, and she the one kneeling, but it's Tansy who's giving me a gift. It's one so shining and pure that I hardly know what to do with it. I've entered into this pact with her trust and been too obtuse to realize what she was handing me.

I have so much fear it threatens to swamp me. Fear and worry that I can't be worthy of what she's giving me. I don't know how to be someone else's lifeboat when I barely know how to steer my own ship. Even now, I don't know how to do this. To guide us from emotion and depth to sex. Because that is what I'm supposed to do, isn't it?

I let myself have this time with Tansy wrapped around me. I fold my arms around her shoulders in return. My spine bends and my shoulders relax. Time marches on, and for once that's okay.

I have Tansy and she has me.

I lose track of how long we hold each other before I tuck a couple of fingers under her chin and tip her face toward me. "Kiss me."

She has to stand up again to do it, but then her mouth is on me. We catch flames with both hands and drag the explosion around ourselves. I think we're both throwing ourselves into the kiss, giving it everything we have, because our mouths—such a simple part of our bodies, the same and yet so different—are the easiest way to explore the enormity that's happened to us.

How long can we hang on to this feeling? How long can it last when the world itself is so impermanent?

I wrap one arm around Tansy's ass and heft her into my hold. She pulls her lips from mine, gasping. "Be careful!"

She's taller than me this way. I have to look up and she's looking down, which means that her curls fall around both of us. "You're tiny. It's fine."

She hitches her legs around my hips, which honestly does help balance her weight. What had been manageable becomes comfortable. Her wrists drape over my shoulders. She nuzzles my temple and brushes little kisses over the shell of my ear. The tickle makes me shiver.

The small room means the bed isn't far away. I toss her down. She flails to catch her balance and then leans on her elbows. The quilted bedspread bounces around her, raising the scent of cheap detergent. She's grinning in a way that lights me up.

"If I'm so little, how come ya needed to throw me down so quick?"

"Because I like throwing you around?" I grab her ankles and yank her across the bed toward me. She squeals. I grab her hip for leverage and twist her onto her stomach. "No, wait. Because I have plans for you."

She's laughing. She pushes to her hands and knees and makes a pretty earnest effort to scramble up the bed. "What plans?"

"Why don't you come back here and find out?" I snag one of her ankles, wishing I had her smooth skin instead of the cool leather boot. When I pull her back, she holds on to the blanket so that it comes with her and exposes stark white sheets.

She doesn't say anything, but she looks back over her shoulder and wiggles her butt. She settles low on her elbows so that she becomes a sinuous curve. I open my palms over her ass, letting my fingers appreciate her structure. Even through jeans, she's soft enough that I only want more.

So I bring one hand back to my shoulder, swing wide, and smack the hell out of her ass.

"Oh!" She jolts, her toes coming together.

"Too much? More?" My breathing is coming hard and fast. That same hand hovers in the air as if it would take flight on its own. I like that. I want to give her more. The sting in my palm has to be half the sting in her cheeks. There's nothing in this entire world but her and me.

If she says it's too much, I'll stop in an instant. This is only good if it's her and me against the world. If it's me against her, it defeats the whole purpose.

She nods. Her hands clench the edge of the bedspread but her hips lift again. "Will you take it slow?"

I would promise her a colony on the moon if she asked for it. Keeping a spanking to a sedate pace seems like something completely within my wherewithal. So the fact that my fingers have a little tremble is absolutely beside the point. "Yes, little one."

"Okay," she says on a whisper.

"There's only going to be ten this time. That's what good girls get."

She bites her bottom lip and lays her head against the bed. "Am I your good girl?"

"The best."

I hold back some for the first smack. Her jeans are a little thin and stretchy, but it'll still be enough to wake her up. The second makes her eyes widen. I keep going at a slow and steady pace, watching her face instead of her ass as I might have guessed I would.

On number six, her eyes flutter shut and she lets her lip free of her teeth. The plump curve is pink and gleaming just enough to drive me crazy. I want to take her mouth, then take her pussy and see which is sweeter. Instead I keep the spanks smooth and even. I can barely feel the heavy thump of my pulse in my pussy. I shift to rub my swollen clit on the inside seam of my jeans. It's not enough but at the same time enough to keep the raw edge off my hunger to get through what Tansy needs.

Spanks seven and eight are methodical. I move around her ass so that the pressure is spread. Nine I land right in the middle of her seat, low enough that the edge of my hand is against her pussy. She jumps and gasps, then just as quickly hides her face against the bed.

"No," I say. "Let me see you."

She comes up on her elbows to look back at me. She's fevered, bright red across the tops of her soft cheeks. Her eyes seem more blue than hazel against her flushed skin. The inside of her bottom lip shows in a pout. "It's a lot."

"That's why you were hiding?"

I can't wait to spank her bare ass. It's not something I'd have previously counted as a must have in a relationship, but with Tansy, it's all different. I rub her clothing-covered butt and even through the material I feel heat coming off her skin.

"This is . . ." Her lashes flutter as she goes somewhere inside herself. "This is intimate."

"It's supposed to be."

She nods. The loose hem of her flannel rides up her back, but her tank top keeps anything from being exposed. In all ways but the truth, this tableau is practically modest. We're both dressed. We haven't even taken off our shoes. "It's good that it is. But it's hard too. My brain races so fast, trying to figure out what you want and how I can respond. How I'm supposed to respond. But then you smack me and all that flies away. For a little while, at least. And I know I'm showing you me. The real me with no way to hide."

"That's possibly the sexiest fucking thing anyone's ever said to me."

She's still bright red, the awkward crimson of an embarrassed blush. "I'm sure you've heard way better dirty talk."

"No. Filthier, sure. But all the fuck-me-harder porn star acts in the world can't compare to the way you open up."

I sink to the bed next to her, one arm around her waist, and I balance her face with my other hand. Her mouth melts as I kiss her. She's exactly as sweet as she should be. Once I give her the last spanking, I'm going to yank her jeans down and make her feel as physically good as I do emotionally. I think that's about four orgasms worth of good. I can work with that.

"More, please?" she says against my lips. "I want my last one. I want to be a good girl. Your good girl."

Maybe she's getting the hang of that dirty-talk thing after all because, Jesus Christ, did that do it for me. "Yes, little one."

I stand, lining myself up behind her at the end of the bed. She makes for a flawless picture. Her ass curves into her soft thighs. I put one hand on the small of her back. Taking a moment to breathe deeply doesn't make my head spin any less.

The words bubble up in my chest first, a hungry and live beast that wants to give as much as it takes. I would claw away the world if I could keep us here, in this room forever.

"Tansy . . . I love you," I say, regretting it and fearing it and wishing that it wasn't so fucking hard as soon as the words come out of my mouth.

And then I spank her.

chapter

Twenty-One

TANSY

*I*t turns out that I'm really, really good at pretending to not hear things.

It's probably how I managed to be with Jody for so long. Why it took seeing her bouncing up and down on a barely legal caterer's penis to break the spell. I can be practically delusional when I want to be.

And, oh, do I want to be.

I smile at my mom across the same dining room table that we've eaten at for my whole life. Nanna Ethel is next to her, plowing through a plate of fried pork chops covered in mushroom gravy. With the way she eats, she ought to be more than ninety pounds. Justin sits next to me, and my dad is at the head of the table. Cai is at the foot.

Cai, who five hours ago said that she loved me.

The dining room chairs are padded across the seat and the back, but my butt still hurts a little bit. Not a lot. Just enough that I feel a sting when I reach for the butter. I hold back my whine.

"You okay?" Justin asks, then takes a bite of Mom's roast chicken.

I could smack the food right out of his mouth. "What? Yeah. Why wouldn't I be?"

His eyebrows lift, and he talks around food tucked in his cheek. His manners have always been appalling. "The horseback ride you took with Beth this morning?"

"Yeah, I can't imagine you've been doing much riding where you live now," Dad says at practically the same time Cai says, "With Beth?"

I cringe. There are two distinct trains of thought going in my head. On one side, I can't handle the jealousy that's about to come my way. I should have mentioned it earlier. It's always easier to diffuse a situation by getting out ahead of it rather than letting Jody—or whoever—get angry and then trying to deal with it.

But at the very same time, this is Cai. She is not Jody. She's not going to freak out because that's just not her way. It spins my brain to have two so different certainties at the same time. I ignore the clench in my stomach and choose the good.

"We went for a trail ride," I say to Cai, before I look back at Dad and try to redirect the conversation. "You're right. There's no room for boarding a horse when you're living in an apartment above a garage."

He shakes his head. He doesn't like where I'm staying now, and he's made no secret of it. "Over a garage. What kind of silliness is that? You should have let your mom and me come out and move you into a real place."

He has absolutely zero concept of how much a "real" place according to his definition costs in my commuting area. And zero concept of what my place is actually like, decorated a la Lowenstein. I hide my smile behind a forkful of homemade macaroni and cheese casserole. "Sorry, Dad. I didn't want to wait."

Mom's got that look on again—the one that's somewhere between annoyed and worried. Two furrows cross her forehead. I have that same expression when I worry. Someday my face is going to be her face in a way that I can't comprehend now.

"You know how I feel about that whole situation," she says, which is pretty restrained for her.

I'm chastised. My smile drops away. I glance at Justin, who's got the same rounded shoulders he'd get when Mom got onto me about my grades at the dinner table, back in my sophomore year. "I know, Mom."

I should have had her there, at the wedding. There wouldn't have been any wait involved then, because they could have gotten my stuff out of the apartment the same day. I might not have ended up trapped on that couch. Though I haven't told Mom about that, I feel like she knows. I've damaged a little bit of her mom-ness by denying her the chance to keep me safe.

Letting Jody manipulate me into not protesting when they declined the invitation is one of my biggest regrets of my life. I push macaroni around on the white plate, all the way up to the pink roses around the border.

Cai pats my knee, then squeezes it. I look up at her and realize that in the space between memories and my imagination, I'd turned her surprise over the mention of Beth into upset with me. But it's not actually there on her face.

She's wearing a baseball-style T-shirt, much more casual than anything she's worn on our dates over the last two months. Her hair is parted down the middle and pulled into a pony tail at the top of her neck. She doesn't actually look that out of place in front of the china cabinet filled with big-eyed porcelain dolls.

And then I remember that she said she loves me.

My stomach clenches hard around the dinner I've managed to eat. I pretend I'm not panicking like mad and smile at Justin instead. "How'd the interview this morning go?"

"Fine." He shrugs. "I start on Monday."

"Justin!" Mom half comes out of her chair with happiness. "You didn't tell us."

"He told me," Nanna says. She beams at Justin. "He killed it at the interview."

"Wasn't much of a challenge. North Traffic takes pretty much anyone who applies." He directs his next words at Cai. "They used to make packaging for CDs. Switched over about a decade ago to these random cell phone accessories. One of our biggest industries in town."

"Be good to get in with them," Cai says.

"Yeah," Justin agrees. "Unfortunately, means I can't take you hunting on Monday."

"Oh man," I say as I put the pieces together. "That sucks. Can we go on Sunday?"

"Beth could take you," Mom pipes up. She's got her mouth shaped into a smile that couldn't melt butter. Dad shoots her a *what the hell* look that mirrors how I feel.

"I'm sure we'll be fine." I had a great time with her on the ride this morning, but that had been Mom's idea too. And it had also been Mom who invited Beth to my homecoming party.

She'd never been against me dating Beth, but she'd never been this keen on her before either.

Nanna's weathered cheeks fold around a smile. "I should take you. Wouldn't that be a gas?"

"Mom, be serious." Mom doesn't find Nanna Ethel nearly as funny as I usually do. "Beth's got her hunting license. Goes all the time. I'm sure she's got plenty of extra equipment."

"They can still use my gear," Justin pipes up. "And my four-wheeler. Tansy's been hunting plenty of times. They'll be fine."

"I'm sure," Mom agrees. She shrugs. That's a dangerous shrug, one that usually accompanies telling Dad that sure, he can go play poker with the boys even though he left the garage a mess, that's fine. "I was just trying to help."

I narrow my eyes at her and decide not to kick her under the table. I have no idea what she's up to, but I don't like it. Nanna catches my gaze, but when I lift my brows in question, she only has a shrug in return.

"It might be a good idea," Cai pipes up.

My jaw drops. "What?"

"I mean, I know you've been hunting plenty of times, but hasn't it been a while?"

"Almost ten years," I have to admit. "Since I last lived here."

She puts a hand out, palm up. A few lines of ink escape the cuff of her T-shirt, curling around her wrist in a colorful streak. "So it might be safer. To have someone who's really up-to-date."

"That's what I was thinking," Mom says with a smug nod. "I'm only looking out for you."

I just bet she is. But I don't see a way out of this corner. I look at Dad, who's kind of confused, but Justin is oblivious as he shovels down the last of his pork.

"Anyone mind if I grab the last one?" He uses his fork to point at it.

"Go ahead, dear," Mom says. "Should I call Beth for you tomorrow?"

"I can take care of it."

"Of course you can, dear," Mom says in a tone that echoes the way she told Justin that he could have more pork. Maybe it's just her and the way she is, and I'm the one making something out of nothing. Justin hadn't thought anything of the tone.

If I hadn't gone away, if I hadn't let Jody take apart the pieces of my life, maybe I wouldn't feel like there's anything weird going on. This would just be part of the fabric of our lives. Mom butting in wherever she liked in a really mom-like way.

I look down at my plate and push my food around a little more. Cai, Justin, and Dad start talking about the upcoming football season. Dad roots for the Packers since there's no Idaho team. Justin naturally followed his lead to the Pack. They give Cai hell for her allegiance to the Raiders—even through their move to Las Vegas.

"I don't care where they play." She pokes the tabletop in emphasis. "They'll always be the LA Raiders. You can't change that."

"Sure you can," Justin says with a grin. He scrubs a hand over his jaw, where he's scruffy. "It says 'Las Vegas' all over their merchandise now. On their website. I'd bet it's on their checks, even."

"You'll never know, will you, Justin?" I tease. I pick up the platter that held the potatoes and stand up. "Are we all done? I'll clean up."

"Well. Yes, I guess." Dad puts his napkin next to his plate and pushes away from the table. "I'll help you."

"Certainly not," Cai says, grabbing the mac and cheese bowl. "I'll do it."

"You're our guest," Dad protests.

"I can do it all myself!" I snatch the bowl away from Cai and stomp toward the kitchen.

Mom always cleans as she cooks, so the gray Formica countertops are already bare. I drop the bowls I'm carrying on one and open the cabinet where the Tupperware used to be kept. Instead of a motley assortment of re-used margarine containers, I stare at a line of pint glasses.

"You okay?" Cai asks quietly from behind me.

I blink away the tears that are burning my eyes. "Yeah. Sure. I don't even know how mom's kitchen is set up, so I'm just peachy."

She holds my shoulders. Her grip is warm and her thumbs rub under my short-sleeved T-shirt. My skin prickles with the good kind of goose bumps.

When she tells me what to do, the whole world goes away. I wish I knew how to take that feeling and bring it out of the bedroom. Even now, I can feel Jody standing between us. I can practically smell her expensive perfume even though I want desperately for her to go away.

"It's not a big kitchen. We'll find it."

She's right. The kitchen is small and the maple cabinets limited. I shrug away from her hold and start tossing them open one by one. Cai stares at me as I move around the square kitchen. I pretend I don't notice, just like I'm pretending that I didn't hear her earlier. I don't find any plastic ware, but eventually I find a stack of glass storage bowls with snap-on lids. I grab a couple and start loading up leftovers.

Cai clears the table and brings things in from the dining room. She scrapes food into the disposal and quietly loads the dishwasher.

We're done too soon. I use a dishrag and wipe down the counters just so I can put off the inevitable. Until I can't anymore. I drape the rag over the edge of the sink, carefully lining up the corners. "Want to go for a walk?"

"Depends."

"On?"

"Whether you plan on ever talking to me again."

I make my gaze meet hers as if my insides aren't shaking apart. "I don't know what you're talking about."

"Where did I screw up?" She takes my hand, then leads me out of the kitchen and through the back door.

The air is crisp. We probably should have grabbed our jackets. Her arms find my shoulders and my waist and pull me near. I keep upright for a minute, then two, but nevertheless, she persists. With one last tremble, I let free the breath I'd been holding and rest my head against her shoulder.

"I don't know how to do this," I whisper.

The cold night snatches my words and throws them to the mountains. Above our head, a quilt of stars stretches. Cai pets my head. I like the weight of her hand across the back of my skull. Everything is so quiet that I can hear the near-silent rub of my coarse strands against each other.

"I'll be honest," Cai finally answers. "I don't know how to either."

Twenty-Two

Cai

It's not the answer she wanted, which makes sense because it's not the answer I'd wanted to give either. One of us ought to be able to keep her shit together, and it really should be the one who thinks she has the right to boss the other around and spank her.

Except no. I'm still pretty much batshit.

Tansy sighs. "Have you ever been in love before?"

"Not until you." I hold her to me when she flinches. "I told you that I didn't do long-term."

"I know. I just . . ." Her words drift off, and she sighs. The puff of her warm breath flows over my neck. "The last person who said they loved me was Jody."

"I'm not her."

"I know," she replies instantly.

Sometimes I wonder if she wants the filthy games we play because they're so very different from whatever she did with Jody. Which makes me wonder if it were just Tansy and me, slow and soft and sweet in bed, would she really know me from her shitty ex? What would it take for her to make love with the lights out?

Christ, maybe I should take it back. Love is dangerous bullshit anyway. All it ever does is get people hurt.

Or hurts the people left behind. This is exactly what I've been terrified of all these years. Until Tansy snuck in under my defenses.

But even as I think it, I don't know how I could shove the words back in the box. This greedy, vibrant feeling is too much to keep in.

I hold Tansy tight. "I don't want to scare you. And I've kind of already scared myself, because I've never felt like this before. Most importantly, I want you to know that you don't have to say anything in return."

She flinches again, but it's more like she's trying to get closer to me than try to pull away, so I don't freak out. I twine my fingers through her hair and tug her head back so that she looks up at me.

Her parents' backyard is huge, and it's obvious that they've lived here for a long time. Everywhere there's the kind of projects that you only get done when you've got a few years on your hands. An artificial embankment is built up with railroad ties. In the south end of the yard is a gazebo that Paul had proudly told me about making with Justin and Tansy both helping him. White fairy lights are strung around the porch awning.

Underneath them, Tansy seems dangerously young. It's the first time the difference in our ages has struck me like this. Her bottom lip is soft and tremulous. "Do you promise?" she asks on a whisper. She's got fistfuls of my shirt at my waist.

"Promise. No pressure," I tell her, even as my heart is crying for some kind of proof that it's not alone. That I'm not walking a tight wire between skyscrapers.

I've been skydiving, I drive a motorcycle; I've swum with sharks. Rock climbing wasn't enough; I had to learn to ice climb. When that wasn't enough, I went up a waterfall in Canada. None of it is anything compared to how I feel right now. There's so much adrenaline rushing through my system that I taste copper at the back of my mouth.

"I'm scared, Cai."

"I know." I make myself strong and tall for her. Brave in a way I'm not sure I'm carrying off. It's hard to hold two people up.

I've been here before. When my sister disappeared and my mother was a ruined wreck. Dad propped her up as much as he could, but Mom had never really been the same afterward. I'd learned to keep my troubles to myself because she couldn't handle them without thinking of Xue.

Just like now. I shove my fear into a little ball and punch it way, way down inside me. There's me and Tansy holding on to each other in the dark. That's enough. If she leaves me, it'll be enough once I'm in the dark on my own.

Dinner was strange and great at the same time. Tansy's family is incredibly nice and genuine, but I didn't realized how much I thrive on Tansy's gaze on me until it was gone. She didn't look at me once. Through me. Past me. Kind of near me. But never at me in the intoxicating way she normally does. I'd do anything to get that back, even if it means acting like I'll be okay if she never loves me in return.

Even though I know that's a lie.

chapter

Twenty-Three

TANSY

The cruddiest part about hunting is how early it starts. It's still dark as I wrap both hands around the ancient metal thermos Mom handed over as we scooted out the door. It's too well insulated though, and I can't get any sense of warmth. My breath hovers in front of me in puffy clouds. The tiniest hint of lightening sky in the east is our only sign that dawn is on the way.

Cai huddles into her jacket, huffing into her clasped hands. "Damn, it's cold."

Beth's showing no sign of the cold. She's tossing gear around in the bed of her truck and pauses and looks down at both Cai and me. Her fists rest on her hips. "Did you layer? You've got to layer up when it's cold out. Not that this is actually cold, but you're both Californians now."

"I layered." I lift an arm, showing how puffy I am. I've got a tank top, a long-sleeved shirt *and* a short-sleeved shirt underneath my blaze-orange sweatshirt. There's no way I'm either complaining about the cold or getting shot.

Cai stomps her feet and shuffles to get warm. "It's going to be in the fifties later. I didn't want to wear too much and get overheated. Besides, I wore a coat. Coat equals warm."

"Drink more coffee," Beth says cheerily. She's wearing camouflage overalls and an orange beanie. She hops down from the truck bed more nimbly than she ought to be able to manage in knee-high wader boots. "Ice fishing. Now that's something you've got to bundle up for."

"Noted," I say. "No ice fishing for me. Ever."

"I'm starting to remember why you moved to California." Beth points a finger at me with a teasing grin. "You're a cold wimp."

"Not having winter for eight years has spoiled me."

Beth hands Cai an unloaded rifle. Yesterday we had a hunter safety class from Justin's buddy Alan, who works for DNR, so I'm not super nervous. Not really. It's weird to see Cai jack open the chamber and double-check that it's empty. She looks too rough and urban to be out here in the woods. Even the jacket she's wearing is stylishly masculine: a slim-line FUCT jacket with double zippers and seaming that emphasizes her height and stature.

I swing the shock-proof case of my camera over my shoulder. My weapon of choice for this outing is my DSLR camera. I could have used the same pink-stock Mossberg that I first went hunting with twenty years ago. That time I'd been with my dad and Frank. They'd joked and laughed, keeping their topics tamed down out of respect for me.

We're a quieter party as we make for Beth's usual hunting blind.

She's being generous by sharing her spot. The terrain has changed so much over the years that I'm an out-of-towner who needs a guide. I know the shape of the pines and the way they stretch toward the sky, but the trail cuts through the underbrush differently.

Deeper in the woods, an animal skitters away. Cai peers into the dark as if she'd be able to see what it is. She controls the direction of her shotgun's muzzle surprisingly well, making sure it stays pointed away from either Beth or me. Alan stressed that safety precautions should be taken at all times, even though she checked that it was unloaded. She's doing it.

"Think it was a deer?" she asks in a half whisper.

"Probably not," I tell her. "Too small. Bunny or fox."

"Fucking cool." The white flash is her teeth. She's smiling, which brings out my smile in return.

It *is* pretty fucking cool. "Nature is awesome."

This is what I'd thought of, after all. The reason I'd decided to invite Cai to Idaho. I knew she'd be this alive and in the moment. She embraces everything with her whole heart.

Including me.

I shake that away. I can't look at it now. We're tramping through the woods following Beth, whose headlamp casts bouncing white light over the path in front of us. If I get too deep in my head, it'll be my luck that I'll wander away from the trail and get lost. Maybe that'd be the answer to all my problems though. No more crazy-in-my-head Tansy if I'm too busy being eaten by a bear.

Beth's homemade box blind is on a small platform reachable by ladder. There's camouflage on the outside with plywood on the inside. It's claustrophobically narrow, with room for three camp chairs lined up and a little space for our gear and not much else. Thank god for the short window that runs almost all the way across the front. It's meant for shooting out of, but it also lets in a little fresh air. At least we warm up pretty quickly.

Waiting as the sun comes up and the forest starts to wake is pretty mind-blowing. The more still we are, the more the leaves of the trees rustle and shift. I sip coffee in slow motion so I don't miss a moment.

"There we go," Beth says in a heated whisper. She points across the clearing. "Here comes mama and her sweetheart."

"Oh, wow," Cai breathes.

I put down my coffee cup silently and scoop my camera out of my lap. Through the zoom of my lens, the quartet comes so close I can count the spots on the fawn. The male of the pack has a small but beautiful spread of antlers.

"He's a five pointer," I tell them. Well within the requirements of our deer tag.

The rustling of fabric next to me says Cai is standing, moving forward to take aim. I get up too and run off a series of snaps before it's too late. The lens whirs but otherwise my camera is silent.

Beth offers advice in a whisper. "Line up your sights with the chest. Breathe slow. Stay calm."

The female deer freezes and looks up in our general direction. I don't think she's spotted us though. It's the wariness of a woman who's been in danger.

I know that look.

"I can't do it," Cai suddenly says. She lowers the rifle.

"You can, it's easier than you think. Look, he's coming even closer."

Beth is right. The buck ambles toward us. He's grazing on tall grass. They're busy getting fat for the winter.

"No, I mean I know I *can*," Cai explains in a whisper. "But I don't want to. It's enough to be here."

I lower my camera and look at Cai over it. She has a wondrous smile, the corners tilted up and her expression relaxed in a way that I normally only see when it's her and me in bed together. And only after we're done, too. When we're playing, she's intense in a way that makes my fingers tingle now in memory.

"What?" Beth is faintly incredulous, and I kind of can't blame her. We got up stupidly early to only make this a hike, plus had to go through the safety class and the money Cai's paid . . . "Do you mind if I do?"

"Go ahead."

Beth is an expert. She's barely lifted her gun and sighted in before the air is rent with a loud crack. Birds caw and flutter through the forest all around us. In the clearing, the mother deer and fawns rear and leap away. I don't even see blood before the buck falls as if his legs have gone boneless.

Cai slowly unloads her weapon, gaze trained on the deer. When she puts it down, I slip my hand into hers. "Are you okay?" I whisper.

She nods, gives me a little lift of her mouth that's kind of more an assurance that she's okay than a real smile. "That was really something," she says to Beth.

"It's not a big deal to chicken out." Beth whacks Cai's shoulder. "We can try again tomorrow morning."

"No, I think I've gotten what I came for."

"Are you sure?" Beth is confused. She glances at me as if for direction, but I just shrug. "You got a license and a tag and everything. I'd hate to see you go home empty-handed."

"No, really. It's fine." Cai shakes her head. "Just looking down the barrel and knowing that I could do it was enough for me. What am I actually going to do with a deer anyway?"

"Well, I know I'm gonna take off and dress it," Beth says with a shrug. "Looks like a nice amount of meat on him. I've got a deep freezer to fill up. If I don't have room, Tricia Pelfer has a chest freezer too."

She heads out of the blind to do the dirty work of preparing the deer. I take the chance to lean into Cai and rest my head on her shoulder. I'm not afraid of PDAs around my old friend, but it had seemed unwise when Cai was carrying a gun. She opens, letting me push under her arm like an insistent kitten, and then holds me close to her side.

"Who's that Tricia?" she asks.

"Single mom. Got three girls and works at the bar." I watch Beth arrange the deer so its hind legs are downhill and its head on a couple of rocks. "I bet she ends up giving most of it to Tricia anyway. Talking about keeping it for herself is just show."

"She's nice."

"Yeah, definitely."

"She's not getting you back."

"What?" I say, laughter making the word come out all weird. "God, no. I can't even— What?"

She rubs my back and looks into my eyes. I wonder if she sees the weird, shifting guilt that I carry on behalf of Mom. It's not that I want Beth back, or even that she wants *me* again, but I have this sneaking suspicion about Mom's planning. What she hopes for me.

And the thing is, I kind of don't mind the idea of never leaving. The air is cold and clean in a fresh way that doesn't happen in Southern California. The cleaner the air gets there, the more it's scented with salt, which is just weird. Here are leaves and grass and clarity I don't get anywhere else.

But in my arms is a Californian who says she loves me. She's a good woman, the kind who can sight in on that antler spread and decide that she doesn't actually have to pull the trigger because she doesn't have a practical use for the animal. The cold has turned the tip of her nose dark pink, which probably means that mine is glowing like Rudolph's.

I lean up on my toes and kiss her. Our cold noses bump. Her lips are cold too, at first, but after a long moment she opens up and lets me into her warmth. I lick into her mouth, and her tongue comes out to meet mine. We taste like black coffee, as if we're part of a pair.

I pull back only far enough to talk. "I promise I have no interest in Beth."

"Good enough for me."

Even this is different in a beautiful way. A way that waters my soul with gentleness. I didn't realize until she said that so easily that even part of me had still expected a worse reaction. But now there's no part of me that's waiting for an interrogation once we get back to her hotel room. I know that's not going to happen.

She trusts me. She loves me, and that love doesn't make her so fragile that she has to treat me like a weapon waiting to be launched against her.

I feel her chest against mine. Her curves and my curves go together. I kiss her again and this one catches fire. She holds my face between both her hands so that she can tilt me to the precise angle she wants. I hold on to her wrists and let her take me wherever she likes. I always know it's going to be somewhere good.

My body is just starting to warm from the inside out when I hear Beth laughing.

"Oh, Jesus," she says. She's come back into the blind for a couple of ziplock bags and paper towels. "God, you two really are like newlyweds or something. Who the hell else would start getting it on in front of a dead deer?"

I jolt away from Cai and cover my face with my hands. "Oh, eeewww," I squeal. "That's nasty."

"You're the one who was doing it." Beth is chuckling at us and wiping her hands on a rag. The brown material doesn't give away much in the way of stains. The rust on her fingers is blood though. "I'm just pointing it out."

"Do me a favor and don't point anything out again. Ever."

"I promise to behave."

We follow her out of the tiny box. I don't know about Cai, but I'm feeling a little awkward again.

Beth grabs a line and ties it to the deer, then uses it to hitch the carcass to a tree and haul it up. "Your mom'll never let me hear the end of it if I'm the reason you don't move back home, after all."

"What?" Cai's voice comes out harsh. I haven't heard anything like it from her before. Her eyes are wide, and she's got her arms crossed over her chest, but I can still see her body clench.

"She said Tansy was thinking about it. Nothing set in stone yet."

I shake my head. "I never said that to her."

Cai knows me better than that. It's part of the problem and the perfection of us at the same time. The straight sweep of her brows lower. She glares at me. "But you are thinking about it."

She didn't even make it a question. She didn't need to. I hold a hand out, but I've got no words to rescue myself with.

Beth looks back and forth between us, her expression opening up. She twists a hank of paper towels. "I've stepped in it, haven't I? Shit, I'm sorry. I didn't think you guys were . . . I mean, it's only been three months since . . ." She trails off. "I gotta go load the buck up. I'll be back with the four-wheeler in a minute."

There's more distance between Cai and me than the few feet between us. She doesn't say anything. My insides are a clenching mess. I can't breathe, but I don't want to make a big deal of trying to get air either. I draw in a long, slow breath, and even that can't fill my chest. I'm too busy panicking to feel anything else.

Finally I can't take the sadness coming off her anymore. "Well?"

"Where would you work?"

"There's an opening at the elementary school. It's public, but . . ." I cup my elbows in my hand. I don't think I could be any more curled in on myself unless I dropped to the ground and turtled up.

"You've looked."

"I . . . It was one quick search . . ." I hear myself trail off yet again, and it's like I'm replaying history. This is who I used to be.

Cai won't hurt me. I don't know what she *will* do, but I know this won't be laced through with acerbic barbs that linger for years and cut away at my self-esteem. She seems sad more than angry. There's no hint of rage radiating from her, turning my spine into water.

I can't do this. I won't. I bring my head up and intentionally straighten my shoulders. "Yeah. I searched. I'm thinking about it."

chapter

Twenty-Four

CAI

Tansy is avoiding me. It's a sneaky kind of avoidance, because it's not like she's icing me out. She still stands next to me, and we're together pretty much all day. First we go with Beth to the deer processor, where we run into some guys that Beth and Tansy both know. They're funny and accepting of both my presence and Beth's in-your-face butchness. Mitch offers us a choice between home brew and a Budweiser. I pick the home brew and it's surprisingly good for someone who'd also drink Bud, with enough hoppiness to keep it interesting.

It's a weird feeling. I laugh it up with the group as we lean on tailgates in the street outside the processor's cooler where we've dropped off the deer to be turned into sausage and leather gloves. They swap hunting stories, and everyone finds it pretty funny that I willingly passed up my shot this morning. Eddie, a tall guy with a handlebar moustache, volunteers that it's probably about how I can't exactly take a whole deer on a plane, and I take the olive branch. Good enough for me that they want to understand; I don't exactly crave their approval.

It's Tansy that I watch the whole time. She's on fire, alive in a comfortable way that says she knows her own skin and where she belongs in the world. The only other time she's looked this relaxed is when I told her to crawl to me.

I've got to admit that I like that version of Tansy's relaxation better. It's selfish of me, I know it. I don't give a fuck. I want to take her home to California.

Except then I feel like the biggest bitch possible, because our afternoon stop is lunch with Tansy's grandmother. Her stooped, white-haired grandmother who wears a sweatshirt with high-fiving kittens on it. Tansy collects her from the small set of apartments one block away from Main Street and Ethel comes out holding Tansy's arm. She's a few inches shorter than Tansy, though it's hard to tell if that's because of her curved back. I think she has a tiny bun knotted at the top of her head, but her cloud of hair is so curly that it's hard to tell how it's held up. Maybe pure force of will.

The café is cute. The counter is wood topped with white, and the floors are a dark maple. The chairs are a mishmash of unmatched origins, but the tables are pretty much all the same. A large blackboard announces the daily specials—with a high emphasis on sandwiches and omelets—and that they proudly serve one hundred percent Kona coffee. There's even bulletproof coffee on the list, which I find kind of surprising for some reason. Through an open archway, I see a room that looks like someone's living room, except it's got multiple comfy chairs instead of couches. A big TV is turned to the Food Network.

When we walk in, there's no one at the counter, but a guy immediately hops up from the back room and hustles out to meet us.

"Hi, Ethel," he says. He's kind of chunky, with a receding hairline even though he doesn't seem that old. "Want your usual red-eye?"

"Not today, sweetheart. Give me a dirty chai with coconut milk."

I double take. Sweet old ladies are supposed to order . . . I don't know, regular coffees that they add plenty of milk and sugar to. She sees me looking and smirks while Tansy orders a mocha. She had seemed like a standard grandma at dinner the other night.

"Up you go," she says, shooing me to take my turn. "This place'll put a shine on any of those Starbucks you've got in the big cities, just you see. Order anything you want. Nicky'll have it."

I tuck away the first smile I've felt since Beth's revelation this morning. "A large latte with vanilla and cinnamon?"

"Powder or syrup?"

"Syrup. And soy milk."

"One horchata latte coming right up," he says with a smirk that matches Ethel's. "Got it. Any food for you guys?"

I laugh, letting my guard down. "Okay, how'd you know that one?"

"We've got Hispanic people in town," Ethel says. She wags a finger at me. "Don't judge us and we won't judge you. Okay?"

"Plus I do have Pinterest," Nicky pipes up. He takes oversized mugs from a shelf beneath the syrups and starts zipping around the espresso machine. The steaming milk is a comforting buzz.

"I make sure all my baristas stay up on the latest." Ethel sniffs and takes the mug Nicky hands her. It's shaped like a panda head. I kind of wish I'd gotten that one.

"This is Nanna's place," Tansy says in response to my confused look. "It's been a coffee shop since she moved to Idaho."

"Back in 1966, that was." She leads the way to the back room, where she takes the remote from the box that's labeled *Do Not Touch*. Guess if you own the place, you're the one who sets those rules. "It was different then. Had just a coffeepot and some homemade brownies."

I open my mouth, suddenly wondering exactly what kind of brownies she was serving in the mid-sixties. I glance at Tansy, wanting guidance, but suddenly I realize that she's still doing that seeing-not-seeing thing. Motherfucker. The wide plank flooring falls away beneath me. "Was it still here? In this building?"

"Sure, sure." She settles into a pink chair that looks soft, but not squishy enough that it'll eat her alive. I know old people have a hard time getting out of furniture sometimes. "Tansy's great-grandfather owned it. When I married his son Harold, I told Harold I wasn't going to be your average housewife. I didn't want to leave Chicago, and if I was going to for him, he had to give me something to do. And here we are." She waves a hand to encompass the building.

The place suddenly seems stiflingly hot. Stripping off my coat makes it somewhat better. Tansy curls up in her chair, tucking her feet under her butt. "I used to come here after school a couple times a week."

"That's because you used Kim as a math tutor when she was supposed to be working for me."

"You didn't mind," Tansy says serenely, then sips her mocha. She'd gotten an *Alice in Wonderland* mug assigned to her, and the Cheshire cat's grin leers at me.

My latte is perfect, even if it's served in a *Don't be a salty bitch* mug, with a drawing of the Morton's salt girl. I'm choosing to believe it's not a dig at me. I guess.

"I was hoping it'd remind Kim that she had a brain." Ethel shakes her head. "Shouldn't have gone chasing after that Reynolds boy. She'd have been better off on her own, even with their daughter."

"Sometimes I think you don't believe in marriage, Nanna."

"It's a fine enough thing for some people," she says. "Others, not so much. I was always the marrying kind."

"Did you and Harold have a good marriage?" I ask. It's hard to hold up my end of the conversation when even innocent questions like this are filled with layers. Tansy still isn't looking at me. I turn my mug around in my hands so that *Salty Bitch* is pointed at me.

"Pretty good. He was a nice man." She smiles wistfully. "Always remembered the important days and picked wildflowers for me. I'd have probably married my first girlfriend if I'd had the opportunity, though."

Tansy chokes on mocha and has to cover her mouth with her hand. "Nanna!"

"What?" Her eyebrows lift. She's proud of blowing our minds, I think. "You don't think lesbians these days have the market cornered, do you?"

I try to imagine what Ethel would have looked like in the mid-sixties. Maybe something like Tansy? I can't quite picture it. I look down at the swirly top of my latte. Let Tansy deal with this one.

"No, Nanna. But . . . you married Grandpa."

"I believe you younguns call it bisexuality." She nestles into her seat. "Big cities don't have a monopoly on everything. Or anything, for that matter."

I'm dying of laughter. "Tell us about the girl you'd have married."

"We went to secretarial school together. Very sweet girl who still lived at home with four brothers, and she was the baby of the family. Her name was Tansy," Ethel says, and Tansy absolutely collapses. She has to set her coffee cup on a table, she's laughing so hard.

She puts her hands on her head as if she's holding in her brains. Her eyes scrunch up as she giggles. "Oh my god, you're kidding right? Mom named me!"

"She liked Tansy very much."

Tansy gasps. "She knew? They'd met?"

"Well, I can't as much say as she *knew*." Ethel taps a finger on her jaw as if she's trying to remember. "Tansy came for a few visits through the years. She became a secretary for a VP at one of the car companies out of Detroit. Never married, so she traveled a lot. Always used to take your mom out to the movies."

"Did grandpa know?"

"Sure, sure, he did. I was always honest with him about my life before him. Just the same as he told me about the girl down in Idaho Falls who he knocked up."

Tansy claps her hands over her ears. "Nope. I'm done here." She drops her hands and looks at Ethel. "Wait, do I have an aunt or uncle out there somewhere?"

"I'm afraid not." Ethel shakes her head. "The girl miscarried. Her and Harold's relationship didn't survive the difficulty, which I suppose is for the best. There's a lot of stuff that has to be weathered in a good marriage. It's not all hot cocoa on the porch and wild sex when the kids leave the house."

Good lord, this lady is a hoot. Tansy is blushing so hard that her skin is positively splotchy. I smother my own laughter. "That part sounds like a good time."

"You can make a good life in this town," she says pointedly.

She's on team Stay in Idaho, I guess. I should have expected that. I'm sure all Tansy's family wants her to move home, and why shouldn't they? Her presence makes my life shinier. They must miss her.

That still doesn't mean I intend to give her up.

Unless I don't have a choice. Unless it's better that she's free.

I stare into the bottom of my cup as if I can use the last dregs of foam like tea leaves and read my future. There's never been a brash choice that I've passed up, but not all of them have worked out perfectly. On rainy days, my elbow throbs to remind me—it hasn't healed right since the fall I took in Guatemala, hiking up the side of Pacaya. Literally breaking my ulna had been worth it to be able to see three volcanoes at once.

I didn't get singed then. I might be burned to ash now. It's the honorable thing to do, letting Tansy go. Holding on to her would be almost cruel, especially after the promises I made in the beginning. I told her that I wasn't a permanent kind of woman, and that she shouldn't rely on me for forever. Those words came out of my mouth. I even said them in a far more rational time than when I said that I love her.

How do I even know what love is? If I truly love her, I should want what's best for the life she's meant to live. And I do. I really do. She fits this town, this countryside. She stood out in California because she's never lost the sweet innocence that came with living in a town where everyone loves her. Hell, no wonder she was ripe pickings for that bitch of an ex. She must have taken absolutely everything Jody said at face value.

Just like she takes everything I say at face value. She doesn't realize that I made my declaration in the throes of passion. It's probably not a real emotion. One day she'll wake up and realize that I've unfairly tied her to me and dragged her back to SoCal and she'll start to resent me. Nothing could survive that.

If Tansy ever came to despise me, I don't think I'd be able to go on. I can't let that happen.

chapter

Twenty-Five

Tansy

Cai is weird as heck for the rest of the day. We take Nanna back to her apartment and go in for a while. Nanna first shows off my baby pictures—which is part of why I'd never pushed Jody to visit. Wherever I go, I get treated to trips down memory lane. They're a blast for me, of course, but it's like I have Jody's ghost sitting next to me and rolling her eyes.

It makes me prickly. I keep checking in with Cai, who says everything's fine. She asks Nanna about different pictures, things like what it takes to get a blue ribbon in barrel racing and what 4-H stands for. She was sad earlier, and that's still there, lurking like a wolf beneath her words, but it's different now. She's sad and . . . wistful?

"It's getting late," I say, and it's kind of true. The sun is going down, at least. This ought to be late for an eighty-one-year-old woman.

"Just a minute, just a minute. I'm almost done with you." When Nanna disappears into her bedroom and reemerges with a photo album I've never seen before, I don't like the direction this is going. "This one I keep in my nightstand."

She's going to tell me it's got pictures of her being a stripper or cavorting on a nudist colony or something, and I'm simply not going to be able to handle it. I always knew Nanna was quirky. She did some of the same thing as other grandmothers in town, like baking really great cookies for the softball team bake sales. But in addition to running the café, she also collected rents from the other shops in the building and from the set of apartments she bought in the eighties.

Everyone knew she was a firm businesswoman. I always admired that about her.

I keep my hands folded in my lap and my spine rigidly upright. I go for totally noncommittal. "Oh yeah?"

"I'm not showing you everything in here either." She's holding the leather-bound album between both hands as she sits in her favorite chair. At her elbow is a small table covered with a white doily she crocheted. Four pill bottles are lined up in a row next to a potted ficus. She flips through the book and draws out a photograph.

"Here you go," she says as she passes it over.

Cai gets it first since she's sitting closest. "Is this you?"

Nanna nods. Her eyes are twinkling and her cheeks are rounded by her smile. "It certainly is."

I lean toward Cai only so that I can see the picture. The woman in it is wearing capri-length black slacks with a boat-neck blouse. She's in profile, looking at the guy next to her, and her super short curls give her the look of a pale Audrey Hepburn. They're standing on rough-hewn steps in front of a doorway. "Nanna, were you a beatnik?"

"For a little bit. It turns out that I like having hot water more than I like living 'the authentic life.' Recognize anyone else?"

The guy is handsome enough, with a strong nose and a decent mouth. He's wearing a plain white T-shirt that could be from any time, but the sharply parted hair is pretty old-fashioned. "That doesn't look like Grandpa."

"Is that . . .?" Cai looks up at Nanna, her jaw gaping. "Is that Jack Kerouac?"

"Such a dish. Such a thinker." She shrugs, and the kittens on her sweatshirt look like their high fives actually connect. "So crazy too, but what can you do?"

"You're badass," Cai says, and I flap a hand at her to shush her, but Nanna is eating it up. "Nah, Tansy. Can't hide it. Your grandmother was a wild child."

"Like recognizes like, don't it, girl?" The finger she points at Cai is gnarled and the knuckles thick with arthritis.

Cai leans back in her chair, folding her arms over her chest. Her long-sleeved T-shirt is shoved up to the elbows, and the position shows off her tattoos. When she narrows her eyes, I shiver a little bit—in a good way. She bares her teeth in a smile that verges on feral. "That mean you want to go out for a night on the town?"

"Not tonight." Nanna stands, and Cai and I both take it as our cue to stand as well. "You two should go now. It's getting dark."

I look out the window, and I'm surprised that she's right. Time got away from us. "That snuck up on me."

"Days are getting shorter. Happens when you're this far north."

Is she warning me? Just making conversation? I don't know how to put my thoughts together, much less dig through her words for deep meaning. When I hug her, it's like holding a tween. She's so tiny. If I moved back home, I could take her out to dinner regularly. She has a standing invitation to Mom's house, but she only ever goes about once a week. Something about not wanting to interfere in her daughter's life, but I think it's more about liking her own space as well. Nanna has always been an independent soul.

In Cai's rental SUV, I stare out the window as she drives the couple of blocks back to the motel. Salmon is so small. Everyone's taken me back with open arms. I missed them. I missed absolutely everyone, all the way down to Mitch and Eddie this morning.

Eddie once threw a wad of paper at me in health class because he'd resented being forced to partner with me for tennis in phys ed. I've got to be delusional for how much I *like* everyone, right? Maybe I'm coloring it all with the exhilarating freedom of actually being able to talk to whomever I feel like. If it had been Jody with me this morning...

But it hadn't been. It was Cai.

I reach across the console and touch her thigh. Through her thick denim, it's not much of a stroke, but I take it. "Have you checked in to your flight?"

"I will later. I'm barely under twenty-four hours, and I'm pretty flexible about seats. Don't care what I get."

Because that's Cai. Laid-back when it counts. She turns the corner into the motel. A new layer of orange and red and brown leaves has fallen across the parking lot. They rustle underfoot when I get out and follow Cai to her room.

She has to lean toward the orange-hued porch light to find which way to put the key in. Night has snuck up on us on silent feet.

I lean against her back. She's layered with sleek muscle, enough that I feel like she could hold me up forever. But that's not fair to her.

I have to learn to stand on my own.

She flips the switch next to the door, which lights only the lamp between the beds, and then she stands beside the TV. She looks . . . different. It's not angry and it's not lost.

I hate that I don't know her every mood. As much as I want to stay in Idaho, I want the chance to know Cai.

"I should pack," she says.

"Probably," I agree.

Neither of us moves. She stares into space. I stare at her. I rub my upper arms, trying to fend off a cold that comes from inside.

"Do you think you'll finish out the school year in California, or will you come back here immediately?"

"Maybe at winter break." I step toward Cai, one hand out, but even though she doesn't seem to be looking at me, she jerks away.

"Have you thought this through?" She drops her brown coat on the room's only chair.

"Some." I run a hand up into my hair, scratching my skull above my neck. I pull first, then twist tight. It's a counterbalance to my tumultuous thoughts, but it's not the same as what Cai gives me. "I know this probably seems impulsive, but it's different than running off to somewhere I've never been."

"I think maybe you were supposed to be here all along," Cai says hoarsely. I wanted her to look at me, but when she finally does, it's like I've been slapped with her pain. Her eyes are dark, but it's the shadows underneath them that look like a wraith is clawing her. "You're a small-town girl. Jody kept you from visiting because she knew she'd lose you."

The air is completely sucked out of me. I make a noise that could have come from an animal. Wrapping both my arms around my waist doesn't feel like it'll keep my emotions from vibrating away from me.

"I'm sorry. I shouldn't have said that."

"It's true. God, it's so true." I can tell because of how desperately I now want to hide. I'm so exposed, and I cover it with a little laugh. "I'm mostly really freaking impressed that you figured it out."

The smile she manages to produce carves deeper the lines that fan from the corners of her mouth. "Not much of a magic trick."

Cai and I are standing on the edge of two separate cliffs and trying to reach each other across the abyss. "Is this goodbye?"

Her heart is in her eyes. She holds the edge of the cheap dresser and clenches tight. "I think maybe it is."

For the first time in a long time, I'm grateful for darkness. The single dim bulb isn't enough to cast light on the misery of this situation. Tears rise in my eyes, and I don't try to blink them away. Instead they crest and spill, coursing over my cheeks. "You said you loved me."

"I do." She crosses the vast distance between us and holds the back of my neck. She's shaking as much as I am. "That's why I have to let you go."

I lift my mouth to hers, and it's the first time I've kissed her instead of the other way around. I don't want to let her go, not in word or in deed. Everything I have gets poured into our kiss. Tasting her isn't enough. I wind my grip in the hem of her shirt, my knuckles rubbing her flat stomach.

I need to see her. She lets me pull her T-shirt over her head. She's close to passive, and I'm close to starving. I love the expanse of her light-brown skin, the way her tattoos mark her and make her.

"You're so beautiful," I whisper.

She runs her hand over my hair. "You are too."

And I notice that neither of us are talking about forever, not anymore.

I curl my tongue over the tip of her full breast. Her nipple is a tight bud. I let every taste of her flesh move through me. My hands open over her back, pulling her closer to me. Our bodies curve together. It doesn't matter whether our shapes fit or not: we're determined to make them fit.

I suck her nipple deep and flick the tip of it with my tongue. She likes that, her hold on my hair tightening a little in response. She's still softer than she's always been with me.

Part of me fears her niceness. I want the bite; I want her strong. But I push her back until she falls onto the bed, and suddenly I'm the one standing above her. She's vulnerable to me.

There's something I love about a woman wearing pants but no top. It emphasizes the female parts of her shape, makes her hips a heavier curve and makes her breasts seem even more generous. I stand between Cai's knees.

She has a small smile tipping one side of her mouth. "What are you going to do to me?"

"Anything I want," I answer, but it's really a cover for the way I'm overwhelmed with possibilities.

She knows what this is. We're mourning a relationship that barely got off the ground, and it's all my fault. Three months is ridiculously soon to invite someone to my hometown—and it's even more ridiculously soon to regret what could have been. There's nothing to say that we wouldn't be sick of each other in three more months. If I'd only waited until Christmas for this trip, maybe it would have been filled with sniping and bitching at each other.

Instead of the kind of vacation that could have been the beginning of forever.

I twist the switch, and the lights turn off, plunging us into darkness.

It's a surprise to breathe easier. This is the best I've felt in the dark in a long, long time. There's still a little bit of illumination coming through the front window, but it's only a wide crack of orange light from the parking lot. The way it bathes Cai makes her into someone from the future. Maybe the future I could have had.

I tackle her jeans, unbuttoning and shoving them down her legs. She helps me by lifting her hips and letting me drag off her boots. It's all confused. I don't care. Once she's naked, I lie down on her. We're together and yet separated by my clothes.

I don't know that I've ever seen her from this angle. Thank god for the dark, the way I can't see the expression in her eyes. I think it might break me. I kiss her and kiss her, letting my elbows find the mattress above her shoulders. My hands stack underneath her head. I stretch my legs out so that they lie along hers. Even then, my toes only go to the top of her feet. I'm smaller than her. Not by a huge amount, but it's enough for the difference to be remarkable.

It's there in the way that I kiss her. My desperation. My wish for things to be different. I pour my emotions into her through the play of our teeth and lips and tongue. She takes it all, but it's just that. She's taking. I want to drive her crazy, I want to make her snap and roll me over and fuck me the way she's done before.

I need to know she'll hate it when I leave.

I kiss my way down her sternum, opening my mouth across the subtle arch of her collarbones. She is tight and strong. I lick her skin. She tastes like salt. We've walked the earth together. She's passed up the chance to take a life, because she's not that type. I let my hands skate over her waist, the tight turn of her ribs. I attack her with the fire of a hundred years I won't have. My lips walk the swell of her breasts, then ski down her fullness.

All this is worship. I wish I could give it to her for longer, but I can't even wait for her to break. I slide alongside her, holding her body close to mine. Her hip fits into the cradle of my pelvis. I force her arm over my shoulder so that she's holding me close.

I open my fingers across her hip, where in the daylight I could see her gun tattoo. She surges up into my touch like a sinuous cat. I pet her and pet her until I'm at the top of her panties, as if it were some big mistake or accident. On some level, I'm still afraid that she'll pull away and tell me to go.

It's because she's not taking charge. It leaves me adrift. I have to trust the way that I want her and trusting myself isn't something I've done much.

I scratch my blunt nails across her crisp pubic hair. She's trimmed short and narrow, but I like that there's enough that I know she's a woman. Not some young girl. She's hot, and when I trace over the seam of her lips, I find her already wet.

My breath catches at the realization. Though she's letting me take the lead this time, no part of her is uninterested. When she holds my shoulder and pulls me closer, I know it's even more true.

She hooks my chin with a finger and tips my face up toward her. The dark is thick, but the light from the parking lot means I can still see the gleam of her eyes. I know she's looking at me. "Think you can make me come?"

She isn't calling me *little one*. "Of course," I say, even as I'm trying to swallow past the stinging lump in my throat.

I spread her wetness wider and wider, working up and down her plump lips. She shivers under certain touches, and I make sure to do those again. This is like learning her all over again. It's different to take her kisses rather than to let her take mine. It's different to push pleasure on her rather than to worship her. And that's what I'm doing—making her feel.

I like it, to an extent. I nestle against her side, her breast within reach of my mouth whenever I feel like it, but for the most part I concentrate on centering her pleasure in her pussy. I delve between her lips to rub her clit, but only for a few brief moments. Then I skirt away to circle her opening, to dip inside with only one finger. Enough to tease. Not enough to give her what she needs.

Enough to give *me* what I need though. The connection with her. The way she moves and writhes. This moment between us will have to be enough to carry me through long nights alone. I need to grow and be myself, but if I'm honest, my odds of finding a partnership like this in Idaho are going to be slim. Slim to nothing. No one will stack up to Cai. No one has her strength and magnetism.

I bury my mouth against her breast to hide my grief. This is what I get. Forever won't be wrapped up in a tidy little bow. Her body echoes the pleasure that I'm giving her. The soft growls she makes turns the air into music as she gets closer to coming.

I keep up what I'm doing, not varying the pattern, but she must want something more because she grabs my hand and holds me against her. I open my eyes, but it's still dark. My breathing ratchets faster, and I think it gets even darker. I look up at Cai, but she's not looking at me. All I see from this angle is the underside of her chin, and she could be anyone.

My skin flashes cold. I try to stay focused on her. The hard edge of her ribs juts into mine. Her skin is so soft. The wetness under my fingertips is luscious, but I can't un-feel the way she's holding on to me, and my stomach flips again, and then she comes.

Saying my name. Somewhere a cat plaintively meows.

I jerk back, scrambling away to the foot of the bed. My breathing is too fast. The darkness spins around me. I want desperately to turn on the lights and prove that it's her, that she isn't anyone else. I'm sobbing.

Oh god, I'm sobbing and I can't stop.

chapter

Twenty-Six

CAI

Tansy is sobbing and she won't stop. Her shoulders curl all the way to her knees. She's wrapped into a ball of emotion in more than one way. The wild snarl of her curls hides her face.

I say her name, but she doesn't hear me. She can't through those gut-wrenching cries. They're hard enough that I see the arch of her spine like lonely islands in a sea of pale skin.

"Tansy," I say again, and I take her shoulders.

She snaps, flailing out at me, smacking me away. She doesn't know how to hit, doesn't know how to make a fist, but the smacks hurt nonetheless. Not in a stinging way, but in what they mean.

"No," she cries. "No, no, no," until it becomes a chant that makes my blood run cold.

I back up, hands held out, then back up farther until I'm barely on the edge of the bed. And then I get off it too, because something tells me that the last place Tansy wants to be is in a bed with anyone else.

"Tansy. Little one. Sweetheart." I use every name I can think of, but none of them are getting through to her. She's lost, and I don't know how to save her.

She folds her hands over her face. Her shoulders shake. Even her toes are trying to curl up toward her bottom. She couldn't possibly get any smaller. I stroke her calf, but that makes her flinch hard, so I pull away again and give her space.

I walk around the room slowly flipping every possible light on. I even turn the TV on, though I mute it, and turn it to the Animal Channel because it's the most innocent channel I can think of.

The box of Kleenex in the bathroom is as rough as sandpaper, but I bring it to the bedside table anyway. I also fold up my softest T-shirt, the Black Flag shirt I've had for almost twenty years, and line it up next to the tissues. I take a spare blanket from the closet and cover Tansy as much as I can without coming into direct contact with her skin. She twists the blanket in both hands and uses it to cover her face, but it's worth it because I think her crying is slowing down.

With an open bottle of water in hand, I kneel at the side of the bed and wait.

I say very little, partially because I'm afraid of saying the wrong thing, but mostly because this seems like a storm that's breaking open. I don't want to get in the way of a hurricane. This is the kind that scrubs the land.

I'm not sure how long it takes her crying to ease. It kind of doesn't matter. I would be willing to wait a century as long as I got to comfort her when it's over. Her great, keening sobs eventually give way to weeping.

When she swipes at her eyes with the back of a hand, I nudge the Kleenex forward so it brushes her wrist. She takes a handful blindly. Once she wipes her nose, it's crimson. Her skin is blotchy and her eyes are swollen.

"I'm sorry," she says, without ever opening her eyes.

"There is absolutely no need to apologize."

"You must think I'm crazy."

"No. I don't."

She shudders. More tears leak from the corner of her eyes and crest her soft cheeks. Her hairline is sticky and damp. She wipes her face as if she could wipe away the traces of her crying, but it's a part of her now. "I think you know."

I don't want to pretend like I don't. "Can I touch you?"

"Oh god." She rolls flat so that she's facedown on the bed. Her hands cover the back of her head. "See? I'm crazy. You think I'm crazy."

"I don't think you're crazy." It's safe enough, so I ease up onto the edge of the bed. "But I don't want to scare you or push you."

"You can touch me," she says, and I'm free to cup the back of her neck. She still flinches, but then eases a little bit. Not much. She's made of barbed wire and knotted twine.

I start small, little strokes down the back of her neck to the top of her shoulders. It takes a long time, but eventually she scoots closer to me and lays her forehead against my knee. The small contact is enough to make my heart break. She's so fragile. I could fold her pieces and rip them up in a way that she'd never be able to put back together again.

"Do you want to tell me about it?"

"'It.'" She presses her face against my leg as if she's trying to burrow beneath me. Her word comes out muffled. I reach farther down her back and pet her spine, then the muscles on each side. "'It.' As if it were only one time."

My heart stutters in fear, but I don't think I let it show in any movement of my body. It's probably good that she can't see my frown, though. "I'm so sorry."

"You and me both." This is a cynical, hard-bitten Tansy that I haven't seen before. I wish I didn't have to see it at all, but I'm glad that she feels safe enough to be all sides of herself.

The C-shape of her spine loosens a fraction, and her knees lower. There's a little more give in her muscles. "When we were in college, she used wheedling as foreplay. It wasn't very sexy, but she'd pout if I didn't give in or if I was busy. Or if I didn't have an orgasm, because then she felt like I wasn't 'invested' in what we were doing. I faked it. Just once or twice at first, but then more, and she didn't notice when I did or I didn't." She stops to take a breath. Her sigh comes out shaky, like a sob.

I don't know what to say. *I'm sorry* would be too little and far too late, and I feel like I should be saving it for the true gut punch that I know is coming. "You did what you had to do."

She looks up, obviously startled. "That . . . that's not what I expected to hear."

I shrug, and I don't stop touching her now that she's given me the chance. "What, did you think I was going to say something shitty about faking comes?"

"It's a straight-girl thing."

"It's a sad thing, whether it's in straight sex or queer." I push her hair back from her face. Her skin is blazing hot. "No one ever goes to bed with someone else saying, 'Gee, I hope I don't come and am able to give a great performance.'"

She gives a sharp, dry laugh and lowers her head again. This time she only lays her cheek on my leg rather than trying to get under me. Having her head in my lap makes me feel warm and trusted. I like the feeling.

"Then came the stage where she didn't really believe in foreplay and just wanted to 'get to the good stuff' right away. She said I'd catch up, and she was right. I got wet enough that it didn't hurt anymore."

I can't help it; I make a growly noise that's not like anything I've made before. "I've got some tough friends. Meet a lot of people when you give tattoos. I'm going to fuck her up."

Tansy clenches my calf. "Don't do that. Don't. I don't want anyone going near her."

It's only the obvious panic in her voice that makes me mutter an okay. But I tuck the idea away for later. Skylar has a mean right hook. Her girlfriend is kind of scrawny but fights dirty.

"It wasn't usually like that anyway," Tansy says, and she sounds so much like she's trying to be apologetic that my rage only gets bigger. But I shove it down further. She needs me calm. "Usually she was the one who wanted to get off, and I'd do things for her."

My stomach flips and churns. "So that's what happened now. When I held your hand."

Her agreement is only a small nod against my lap. Then she shudders. More tears leak from the corners of her eyes. Her long, thick lashes are matted together and spiky. She clings to me, and I do my best to be her rock.

It's not a position I've been in before. I'm the one who leaves. Who scatters and runs, fearful of a past that haunts my choices. But I don't have those fears anymore. Tansy might leave me one way or the other, and with this talk of moving home it seems even more likely than *might*. But that's okay. She deserves to have someone who'll hold steady for her.

I rub her back and cup her shoulder. "It'll be all right. Everything's going to be okay."

Even if I don't know how to make that happen.

chapter

Twenty-Seven

TANSY

*I*t's somewhere around three in the morning when I wake up. Cai is at the sink outside the toilet, brushing her teeth using the light from her phone. I sit up and wrap my arms around my knees. "I didn't hear your alarm go off."

She stops brushing, and I think tries to look at me in the mirror above the sink, then she turns around with her toothbrush still in her mouth. "I didn't sleep, so I turned it off a couple minutes before it would have gone off."

"Oh."

We talked until midnight. Mostly I talked. Cai offered me comfort and held me. Somewhere around nine she'd ordered pizza from the place down the street, and the remains of our dinner are scattered around the floor. My mouth tastes like late-night bad decisions.

I'm wrecked. My shoulders and my chest hurt in an actual sore-muscle kind of way. I rub my upper arms. The room feels cold.

Cai flips on the light in the bathroom area, and it's enough to let me see that she's already packed. She's been up and moving around for a little while now.

Getting ready to leave. That's what she's doing. I force myself to think it, to actually run my thoughts over the concept and let it catch at rough edges. "I kept you up too late."

"No such thing." She comes to me and stands next to the bed. She tucks my hair back over my shoulder. "I'd have stayed up all night with you."

"You did stay up all night! And I washed out on you."

"You can't have it both ways." She grins at me. "Did you keep me up too late or did you pass out too early?"

"Shuddup," I mutter, pouting at my lap. "It's early. I'm not supposed to be up at this hour."

"I didn't mean for you to be."

"You were just going to, what? Write me a note?"

"No." She looks so sad. It's in her eyes and the flat hold of her mouth. "But I was going to kiss you goodbye right before I had to leave."

I don't like this. I don't want us to separate like this. It seemed too complicated and not really worth it to book our flights together on the way back when we weren't coming out at the same time. I'm not leaving until tomorrow, and my mom is going to drive me to the airport. It didn't seem like a big deal, because of course we'd have plenty of time together in California.

Truthfully, I kind of wanted to travel on my own. There are a lot of things on my "by myself" list that need checking off. I liked it. Sliding through the clumps of families and darting around weary business travelers to grab the last open seat in the waiting area. I have a feeling I'm not going to feel so much like a sophisticated traveler on my way back. It'll be all wiping my tears away with cheap napkins and eating my feelings with overpriced airport nachos.

I pick at the blanket. "I'm sorry about last night."

"Don't apologize." She holds my hand and laces our fingers together. "There is absolutely no place I'd have rather been."

"Right. Because you adore having your girlfriend freak out in the middle of sex with a mental breakdown."

"If that's what you needed. If it was cathartic."

"Don't leave." My fingers clench on hers, and I grab her thigh with my other hand. "Please. Don't go. I'll buy you a ticket back tomorrow, and we'll drive down together."

She shakes her head with more of that damned sadness. "I have to go."

"You don't. You can call Skylar and tell her you'll be in tomorrow."

"You need me to go."

"No!" I sound panicky again, but that makes sense because I am panicking. She's going to say goodbye and really mean it. "I love you. Stay, please. Move here with me."

"I can't do that."

"You can have a spot in Nanna's building." I scramble to my knees, clutching her waist as if I could physically keep her here forever. "You'll be the only tattoo artist in town. The tourists will die for it. You'll get all the business for miles."

"Hush, little one." She holds my head, and my eyes feel so heavy. I lean into her touch. "Shhh. I'll see you in California."

That's not a yes. I can hear her no echoing in the vast gulf between us. "Don't leave me."

My voice breaks when I start crying. My tears are hot enough that they scorch my cheeks. I think it's because I cried so much last night. I wipe the drops away with the back of my wrist, and then I have to wipe snot away too. Oh god, how puffy and red must I be? Maybe that's why she's saying no.

"You have to do this," Cai says. "This move is something you need, and you need to do it for just you. All by yourself."

She's right. I know she is. The truth only makes me cry harder. I sob and cover my face with my hands as if that'll keep me from embarrassing myself. It's too late. "I'm sorry. I should have never walked into your booth. I've only brought you headaches."

"Don't say that." She drops to her knees beside the bed and suddenly her head is at my waist when she wraps her arms around my hips. "You're the best thing that's ever happened to me. You shine so bright, Tansy. I don't think I've ever met anyone stronger than you."

"I'm not strong," I insist. "I wouldn't have . . . I'd have left so much earlier."

"You did leave. That's what matters. And you're brave and hopeful enough to pull up stakes on your entire life."

"To go back home." Her hair is silk between my fingers. "That's not bravery. That's running away."

"I don't think so."

"I don't want to leave you."

She stands up slowly. The kiss she presses to my forehead stops my tears but breaks my heart.

"You're not," she says. "I'm leaving you."

chapter

Twenty-Eight

TANSY

*L*uke Bryan is excellent packing music. He's telling me about the time that he lost his girl as I fold brown paper around my dishes. I took advantage of Cai running out for lunch and drinks as a chance to crank the country. She's not super fond, though she tolerates the songs of betrayal with a faintly amused smile—and I think I caught her humming a Florida Georgia Line song under her breath a few days ago, though she denies it. Vehemently.

There's not much to pack, since I never really got around to really *unpacking*, so Cai and I figure we'll be done by the end of the weekend. Imogene is coming later in the afternoon, once she's done with the baby shower she's at. The extra set of hands will help. The moving truck arrives Monday morning, and I want everything absolutely ready to go. The less I need the movers to do, the more money I save. The more money I save, the bigger a down payment I have for a house in Salmon. If I play my cards right, I should be able to keep my mortgage far under a grand.

When there's a knock on my apartment's front door, I don't even bother to turn around. It's got to be Cai. "Come in!" I call, then put the paper-wrapped plate in a box.

"This is cute," says a voice that I've often thought about but not actually heard in months.

I spin. The sheaf of paper drops from my numb fingers and swirls around my ankles.

Jody's cut her hair pixie short. I wish it looked awful on her, but it doesn't. It makes the stark ridges of her cheekbones look even more wickedly sharp. She fingers the lights strung on my miniature Christmas tree. Cai gave me the shotgun shell strand almost six weeks ago as an early Christmas present.

"You always did like kitsch," Jody says dryly. "I think it's the diner-loving redneck in you."

I want to rush her and snatch my tree into a hug. Jody only decorated for holidays when it was color coordinated and tasteful. I don't even like her looking at my adorably Charlie Brown–esque tree. "What are you doing here?"

"I wanted to let you know that I've taken you off my insurance policies. You're no longer my beneficiary."

"So?"

"I thought you'd like to know."

I think she might be implying that I'm a money-grubbing whore. Or something. I fold my arms over my chest and cup my elbows. I don't remember what it feels like to breathe. "Okay. That's set, then."

"I just need you to sign this." She pulls a folded pack of papers from the Tory Burch purse dangling from her shoulder. When she smooths them out on the table, they're a thin sheaf of legal papers.

"No."

"You haven't even asked what it is." The coldness she's giving off used to be the kind that froze me and made my blood thicken like ice floe.

"You can leave it, and I'll have my lawyer look at it."

"It's a quit claim on my condo." She narrows her eyes. "You can't possibly think you have any claim on it."

"You're the one who brought me papers to sign." I swallow. My voice is shaking, making mince of my hard-sounding words. "I think that means that you're worried I do have a claim."

"It's always been mine."

"You made that more than clear. You never let me be comfortable there." Jody had gone house hunting on her own. I didn't even see it before she made an offer. I never picked paint, never picked furniture. I was an eternal guest in my own home. Except . . . "It's because I paid most of your down payment, isn't it?"

"That was a loan, and it was repaid by letting you live with me rent-free."

The money had come when Grandpa Harold died. I hadn't thought of it much because it was all wrapped up in the time that he died and when I quit my public school job. Jody let me stay with her free of charge until I started at Woodbridge. She'd just asked me for a loan. "I was your girlfriend."

"You were." She comes closer, and suddenly even having the dining room table between us isn't enough. "I miss you, Tansy."

"Don't say that." I hate that my voice goes up. I hate that I jump back.

"It's true."

"I don't care."

She's close enough to touch me. She grabs my shoulder. Her fingers are ice, which makes me shudder, but even that doesn't make her let go. She drops to her knees.

"Take me back, Tansy. Please. I miss you." She ends on a sob, and her face looks as if it should be crying—her mouth turned down and her forehead wrinkled up—but there's absolutely nothing in her eyes. They're dry. I knew she loved that condo, but this is crazy excessive, even for her.

"Let go of me!"

She loops a hand around my knee and with the other reaches for my hand. I yank away hard enough that I stumble. My elbow smashes a box, and it clatters. I catch the small of my back against the edge of the kitchen counter.

She's saying my name, over and over, and she keeps fucking reaching for me, saying, "Please!"

I kick. It's barely more than a flail. I miss. "Go away!"

She throws herself back, exaggerated shock written on her face. "What the fuck is wrong with you?"

"Don't come near me." I'm half-standing, half-leaning against the counter. My grip is the only thing keeping me from falling. I refuse to go down. My flip-flops skitter across the tile. "Get the fuck away from me."

She holds both hands up as if she's the victim here, as if she's showing me how harmless she is. "I'd never hurt you."

"You raped me." I push myself up and stand. My back aches so damn bad. I don't let any of it show. "On the couch. You hurt me and you raped me and it wasn't the only time."

"That's . . . That wasn't . . ." She stands up.

God, she's taller than me and this kitchen is so small. All the air is gone, because I can't seem to breathe. I'm trying though. I'm learning how to breathe. "It was. It was you, making sure you had power over me. But you know what, Jody? You don't. You'll never have power over me again."

"You fucking bitch," she snarls, and it's as if there's a beast who's been lurking under her pretty face that finally claws its way free. Her mouth is twisted. Her eyes are dark. There's a dull red flush across her cheeks. Her hands clench and open. "You fucking white trashy country cunt. Fucking mountain people. You're lucky that I ever paid attention to you in the first place."

"Oh yeah?" I say, as if my hands aren't shaking and my stomach isn't threatening me with vomit. "Then why were you the one on your knees begging *me* to take *you* back?"

She snaps. Lunges for me. I duck, but there are boxes in the way. She grabs my wrist and pulls and I don't freeze—I grab something out of the open box beside me. It's wrapped in paper but it's hard, and I smash it against the side of Jody's face, then again. One more time as she comes closer instead of going away.

The third time I hit her, the thing I'm holding crashes against her nose. Both crumple. I think I must have been holding a glass, because it loses parts of itself and something sharp slices my finger.

But Jody claps both hands to her face and howls. Blood spurts from between her fingers. "Help me."

"Fuck no." I stand. My hand doesn't hurt. I wonder if it will later. Or tomorrow. Everything's kind of blurry right now. "Get out. Get out of my house. Get out of my life."

"I need help."

"I'll call the cops."

"And I'll tell them you assaulted me!" I think I'd be more scared if her words weren't a mushed-up nasal mess.

"You're the one in *my* house."

"And she's got me too." Cai stands in the doorway, a six-pack dangling from her fingertips. "I'll back her up."

Cai's tank top shows off the way her shoulders and arms are covered in tattoos. Her dark eyes are blazing. Her mouth is set in a flat line. She is so fierce that Jody looks like a baby in comparison.

And I'm just as fierce as her. My shoulders are back and my chin is up. "Get out," I tell Jody. Once upon a time, all I wanted in the world was to go away. It was the only way I could save myself. Now I have a life worth saving, and it's Jody's turn to go away. "I know your bosses. I know your family. I'll Facebook message every single one of your friends and tell them how you raped me. Unless you leave right now."

"Don't do this," Jody says, but her eyes are so wide that I can see the white around the color.

"Don't push me."

Her mouth opens, then closes.

And then she leaves. Breaks and runs, pushing past Cai and battering shoulders. Cai isn't shaken though. She stands firm until the door slams behind Jody, and then she drops the beer. It crashes and foams, but I have Cai's arms around me and I suddenly realize I'm crying.

I break into sobs, but it doesn't feel like the other times I've cried about this. "I'm safe," I say, "I'm safe."

"You are." Cai's hands coast over my back. I think she's holding me in and making sure I'm all right. I can't seem to get close enough to her. I fist her tank top at her waist and push my face against her neck. "I've got you."

"She raped me." I say the words against her skin. My hand hurts, and yet I've never felt more alive in my life. I'm so free. Jody doesn't own even a little bit of me anymore, not even the parts that hide in the dark. "The last night. Other times. She was . . . she was . . ."

"She was a fucking cunt."

I burst into laughter. "Yeah, I guess."

"I know it." She's practically growling. "Jesus, Tansy. You're so brave. I was so goddamn scared when I saw the car downstairs, and you'd already beaten the shit out of her. I can't believe how brave you are."

"I'm not. I'm so weak."

She holds both sides of my face and makes me look her in the eyes. "You are brave. It's why I love you. You're still soft, that's what makes all the parts of you. That's why you're so amazing."

I have no words. Tears spill over my cheeks, and I think they're washing me clean. I kiss Cai. She kisses me back.

I don't know where we can go from here. Cai and I live two different lives, and I need to go home to Idaho. It's where I'm supposed to be. But I know that no matter what, I'm better for having Cai in my life.

I used to think that I knew love, but that was just desperation and loneliness and dependence. This is new. This is strong.

I'm the one who's grown. I'm the one who's done the work to build myself up from the tiny speck I used to be—but Cai has held my hand through the whole process. And I love her. I love her more than I ever would have thought possible.

I don't know what my world is going to look like without her.

chapter

Twenty-Nine

TANSY

By mid-July, I'm intensely glad that I budgeted the money for a riding lawn mower. We had a record rainfall this spring and still lots of rain this summer, and as much as I love my little house, I think I might hate it if I had to walk to mow an acre and a half. Living on the very outskirts of town has its ups and downs. At night, when I can stand on my back porch holding a glass of wine and see the stars stretch until the mountains reach up to claim them? Completely worth it.

Even with the machine, I'm sweating as I park it in my garage and let myself into the kitchen. I strip off my soaking-wet T-shirt and walk into the kitchen wearing only a sports bra.

Gyoza twines around my ankles. "Who's my pretty," I coo as I scratch behind her head. She holds still long enough to stick her orange butt in the air, so I scratch it too. "Who's my sweetie?"

She only purrs in response.

"I don't get a meow?"

She sniffs and wanders away to sit next to her food bowl, which is still totally full. Her nose goes into the air to express her disdain.

"Well, too bad," I tell her. "You're getting pretty plump. The vet said you needed the light stuff."

I'm turning into the crazy lady who talks to her cats, but I'm good with that. I put a load of laundry in, then bring my pitcher of sun tea in from the porch where I'd had it brewing on the wide-board railing. I know it technically doesn't make the taste any different, but iced tea that's been cooked by the sun makes me happy inside and out. I pitch the tea bags and pour myself a glass over ice to take to the papers I have spread over my dining room table.

The room is on the small side, and I don't like the closed-in feeling. If I have a chance someday, I think I'm going to have the wall between the kitchen and the dining room taken out. Or at the very least have the door made into an archway. But at least the window looks out only on the thick screen of trees that hides me from my neighbors.

Not that I've gone full hermit. I know my neighbors on both sides—hard not to in a small town. Patsy, my neighbor to the north, came over to introduce herself with a loaf of poppy seed bread the day after I moved in. Norm came the next day with a list of local service people and a bottle of wine, though he spent most of his time asking me about Patsy. I think I might have the widow and widower over for dinner sometime.

Not today, though. I'm teaching summer school—low teacher on the totem pole—and I've got a stack of assignments to go through. Switching from my small, intimate class of second graders to teaching middle school language arts has been a pretty big jump, but I think I'm covering ground pretty well. Wrangling twenty-five students at a time has been the biggest adjustment. It helps that they're pretty good kids.

An hour passes before I realize, and my watch beeps to remind me to stand up and stretch. I put down my purple marker with a sigh. Anthony is going to need some extra help with his grammar if he's going to pass this time around. Maybe I should call his mom and see if he can stay after tomorrow.

I wander into the kitchen to pour another glass of tea and stand in front of the cool air pouring out of the fridge. My phone is on the counter. I flick the display on, even though I know it won't show me anything good. No messages.

No calls either.

I lean on the counter and stare at the glassy rectangle, chewing on my bottom lip.

Cai's been pretty quiet over the last week or so.

She always answers my texts, and the night before last we had a two-hour talk. But even that had been kind of strange—she'd ducked the idea of a video chat. I mean, yeah, she'd blamed it on her internet, but she didn't even reset the router or anything to try to get it going.

I wonder if she's getting tired of a long-distance relationship.

My stomach flips hard enough at the thought that I put a hand on my tummy as if I could hold my insides still. Terror streaks down my spine and turns my palms clammy.

I immediately pick up my phone and text her. *Hey, lady. How's things?*

I force myself to put it back down and start putting together a salad for dinner. A watched pot never boils and a watched phone never vibrates.

I have the carrots on top of my baby spinach when her reply comes in.

Kind of fired. Will call you tune.

A second pops up almost immediately. *Sorry, using Siri. Tired. Will call soon.*

Oh. Well. I'm sure she doesn't mean that the way I'm taking it. There's tons of reasonable reasons for using Siri instead of doing your own texting. But she's never mentioned it before, and I can't help but feel more weight in the change than in the act itself. She's thinking of me differently, just when I miss her more than I can say. I ache for her. She's bored of me.

That's a change. Crap, a seriously sucky one.

I put my phone away and make my salad with shaky hands.

Cai had been right: moving back home was one of the best decisions I've made in a long time. I thrive in my own house, and I feel so much more comfortable teaching regular kids instead of astoundingly privileged ones. I'm making more of a difference. My family has pooled around me in a way that makes me smile every day. I get to take Nanna to dinner every Tuesday night, and I'm her chauffer to Mom and Dad's house for Sunday dinners.

I belong here. Time in California can only be visits from now on.

Except California is where Cai lives. We've talked about her moving, but only in a vague way. With lots of maybes.

And if neither of us is willing to budge, it'll mean we stay long-distance forever. Except maybe forever is going to end a lot sooner than I thought if Cai's weirdness over the past two weeks is a sign of things to come.

I only manage two bites of my salad before my stomach clenches in revolt. I put it down on the box that's serving as my coffee table. I'm going to have to buy more furniture eventually. Gyoza slinks around the edge of the couch as if I might give her the tuna off the top.

"You don't want it," I tell her. "You don't like balsamic dressing."

Talking to the cat feels a whole lot less cute than it did a couple of hours ago. The house is so damn quiet that I can hear a truck rumble down the street despite my quarter-mile-long driveway.

No, wait. It's getting louder.

I go to the front door and step out, closing it behind me so that Gyoza doesn't get out. It's a truck, but not a big Ford or Chevy like I expected. It's a moving truck.

A moving truck.

I'm starry-eyed. Absolutely psychotically insane. If that's not Cai, if that's some stranger who's gotten lost and is looking for directions, I'm going to throw myself down in my fresh-cut grass and simply die.

The truck lumbers to a stop. The sun slants across the giant windshield, and even when I lift a hand to my forehead, I can't see in.

The door opens. A boot appears first, below the bottom edge of the door, then a leg in dark-gray trousers, and then Cai's shutting the door. Cai. My love.

I'm off the front steps like a shot, running so hard that I'm pumping my arms to go faster. My bare feet smack against the cement walkway. Cai throws her arms wide, and I launch into the air.

She catches me. She always will, I know it.

I wrap my legs around her waist and my arms around her shoulders. Cai spins us. The summer air swirls. My hair is tangled around both of us. I have my face against her neck. She smells like healthy sweat.

"You're here," I say. I'm giggling, and I have tears burning their way down my cheeks too. I lean back enough to look at her. "You're here."

"I'm here, little one." She looks fantastic, if a little tired. There are lines under her eyes and alongside her mouth. "It's a long drive."

"That's a moving truck!"

Her chuckle warms me from the inside out. "With all my worldly possessions inside too. Bike and everything."

"You didn't tell me anything. I was weirded out. I thought maybe you didn't love me anymore."

She lets go of me only enough that I can slide down her body to stand on my own. She holds my face tightly, as if I would dream of looking away from her right now. The fire in her dark eyes makes my toes curl against the hot asphalt of the driveway.

"I love you, little one." She says the words like a vow. "I couldn't stand being away from you anymore. I missed you too much."

"I missed you too." I spread my hands wide across her shoulders and her waist. She's so strong. "I can't believe you're really here. I've dreamed about this so many times."

"I hope that means I won't need my backup plan," she tells me with a smile that's growing. Her hair is down across her shoulders. It shines like onyx under the summer sunlight.

I've known this amazing woman for almost a year. It's hard to believe that much time has flown by, but I think I've needed it. In order to be able to fly, I've had to let my feathers grow in. "What backup?"

"Nanna's going to rent a storefront to me at a cut rate. Says she'll trade me six-months rent if I put a skull on her shoulder."

I laugh. "Oh my god. Mom will kill you if you do that."

"She said we could keep it our secret." She threads her fingers through my hair, holding me firmly in place. "But she also said I could rent one of the apartments in her building if I need to. Do I need to, Tansy?"

I want to say no. I want it with every bit of me, except the little scrap that has learned to stand up for itself. When I catch my bottom lip between my teeth, I bite it hard enough to make myself wince, but I need the little hit of courage it gives me. "Give me something more flowery than that."

For a long, heart-pounding moment, I think maybe she isn't going to do it. She'll tell me I'm silly, and I'll probably cave and tell her that I was just teasing. Just kidding, not really. That kind of thing.

Then she takes both my hands in hers and steps back far enough that she can drop to one knee. My chest squeezes five inches tighter and my lungs are working overtime. The edges of my vision go a little bit gray, but I freaking refuse to faint. There is such a look of ardor and love on her face that I can hardly look back at her—except there's no way I can look away either.

"Tansy Gavin, you're it for me. I don't know how you're you. What you've been through would have crushed another woman, but you came out of the fire forged in steel and yet still as soft as velvet." Her voice breaks a little, and tears pool at the corners of her eyes. I've never seen Cai cry before. It's disconcerting and more tender than I could have imagined, both at the same time. "When Xue was taken from us, I let it harden me. I've been alone a long time because it was safer to be that way. Your sweetness humbles me. Will you have me?"

"You left me." I didn't mean to bring this up. Didn't mean to travel down this road again. "In the hotel room, when I asked you to stay."

"I did that because you were scared that I wouldn't come back." She kisses my knuckles, one hand after the other. Her mouth is a soft butterfly. I think Cai's touch could rouse me from a thousand deaths. "And it hurt. I wanted to stay. I've told you that, little one."

"I know."

"I could barely tear myself away from you." She looks up at me from under her dark, straight brows. "I cried so hard on the plane that the flight attendant brought me a packet of tissues and a free glass of wine."

"You didn't tell me that." I know I sound kind of accusatory, but I can't help it. "I thought we'd talked about it all. But you hid it?"

"Because I didn't want to make you responsible for my pain."

"I'm not responsible. But I'm in this relationship with you. If we're going to do this, you're going to have to trust me to hold my own weight."

Her mouth quirks into a little smile. "See? This is what I'm talking about. You're amazing."

"Are you teasing me?"

"One hundred percent not." She reaches into the pocket of her trousers and pulls out a ring. It glitters sharp and cold. The diamond in the middle is radiant cut in a way that makes the rectangle shape shimmer even more. A handful of smaller diamonds circle it, set in beautiful rose gold, so that the whole thing has a vintage look. I love it.

I would never, ever admit it, but I've scrolled through rings on a dozen sites, always late at night, in the dark, and on my phone. With my privacy browser on. This is the style I wanted and Cai has picked it. She knows me. Knows my taste.

And I'll have so much lace on my dress that I'll look like a goddamn doily.

"Tansy Gavin, will you marry me?"

"Yes," I breathe, almost too quietly. I can barely hear my own voice, and I have to clear my throat. Only moments ago, I could have sworn that I was close to tears. Instead laughter bursts from me, strong enough to lift me onto my toes. My words come out louder this time. "Yes, Cai. I want you forever."

"I'll keep you forever and a hundred years."

When I hold out my hand, Cai slips the ring onto my finger. It's cold at first but rapidly picks up my heat. My jaw falls a little as I stare at my hand decorated like this. A way it'll be decorated forever. It's astonishing and humbling, and I'm happier than I think I've ever been.

She surges to her feet, taking my mouth with hers.

The kiss is hard enough to bend my neck back. I fold my arms around her shoulders and let myself melt. Cai will never let me go. She'd never let me fall, and she'll never try to hold me down either.

Together, we'll fly.

Explore more of the *Belladonna Ink* series:
riptidepublishing.com/titles/universe/belladonna-ink

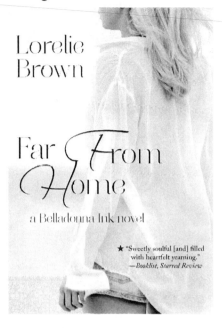

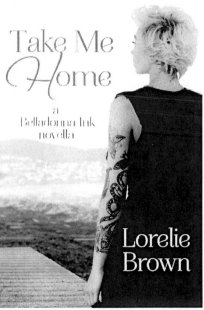

Dear Reader,

Thank you for reading Lorelie Brown's *Her Hometown Girl*!

We know your time is precious and you have many, many entertainment options, so it means a lot that you've chosen to spend your time reading. We really hope you enjoyed it.

We'd be honored if you'd consider posting a review—good or bad—on sites like Amazon, Barnes & Noble, Kobo, Goodreads, Twitter, Facebook, Tumblr, and your blog or website. We'd also be honored if you told your friends and family about this book. Word of mouth is a book's lifeblood!

For more information on upcoming releases, author interviews, blog tours, contests, giveaways, and more, please sign up for our weekly, spam-free newsletter and visit us around the web:

Newsletter: tinyurl.com/RiptideSignup
Twitter: twitter.com/RiptideBooks
Facebook: facebook.com/RiptidePublishing
Goodreads: tinyurl.com/RiptideOnGoodreads
Tumblr: riptidepublishing.tumblr.com

Thank you so much for Reading the Rainbow!

RiptidePublishing.com

also by

Lorelie Brown

Belladonna Ink series
Far From Home
Take Me Home

Jazz Baby
Catch Me

Waywroth Academy
Wayward One
Indiscreet Debutant

Pacific Blue
One Lesson
Riding the Wave
Ahead in the Heat

Writing as Katie Porter
Fireworks (in the *O Come All Ye
Kinky* anthology)
Come Upon a Midnight Clear
Snap

Vegas Top Guns
Double Down
Inside Bet
Hold 'Em
Hard Way
Bare Knuckle

Club Devant
Lead and Follow
Chains and Canes

Command Force Alpha
Own
Bind

about the

Author

After a seminomadic childhood throughout California, Lorelie Brown spent high school in Orange County before joining the US Army. After traveling the world from South Korea to Italy, she now lives north of Chicago. She writes her California-set books because she hates that winter exists.

Lorelie's contemporary romance *Far From Home* is a bronze winner in the Foreword INDIES and was nominated for a Romance Writers of America RITA award. To stay up-to-date on her new releases, sign up for her newsletter at eepurl.com/VdlAz. She promises not to spam you and to only sometimes send you pictures of her shih tzu and yorkiepoo.

In her immense free time (hah!) Lorelie cowrites award-winning contemporary erotic romance under the name Katie Porter. You can find out more about the Vegas Top Guns and Command Force Alpha series atKatiePorterBooks.com or on twitter at @MsKatiePorter.

You can also contact Lorelie on Twitter @LorelieBrown or on Facebook at facebook.com/lorelie.brown.

Enjoy more stories like
Her Hometown Girl
at RiptidePublishing.com!

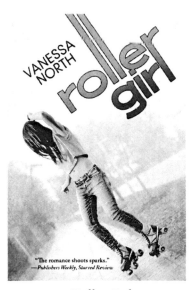

Roller Girl
ISBN: 978-1-62649-418-3

The Butch and the Beautiful
ISBN: 978-1-62649-436-7